Johnny Farrell's Journeys

by

Ronald (Dutch) Hopwood

Johnny Farrell's Journeys

by

Ronald (Dutch) Hopwood

Press-TIGE Publishing
Catskill, New York

For information:

Press-TIGE Publishing
291 Main Street
Catskill, NY 12414
http://presstigebooks.com
Presstige9@aol.com

First Press-TIGE Edition 2000
Cover and book design: Drawing Board Studios

Printed in the United States of America

INTRODUCTION

Destiny grants us our wishes, but in it's own way, in order to give us something beyond our wishes.

—Johann Wolfgang Von Geothe

The mid-nineteenth century was a restless and uncertain time for our country. Famines, wars, and economic depressions across Europe brought an influx of immigrants to our shores. This, combined with economic hard times at home and the discovery of gold in California, created what has come to be known as, "The Great Migration."

Thousands headed for Oregon looking for land to farm and support their families. Others hoped to find gold and get rich quick in California. The great movement inspired the writing of charming lines and verses which encouraged imaginations. Few of the inspired had themselves been west of St. Louis and had little knowledge of the risks in the wilderness beyond. Immigrants, waiting at jump-off points such as St. Joseph and Independence, Missouri, knew even less of the dangers. Those who had been advised accepted it as only hearsay or exaggerated claims, or were too desperate to let adversity stop them.

Many diaries were written on the trail that recorded forever the hardships and heartbreak of their journeys. Each member did his or her duty without complaint and took the hardships in stride. The fortunate among them realized their dreams and found a new life for their families. The less fortunate buried their families along the way.

As with modern day youths, the imaginations of the young of that time were encouraged by stories and rumors.

In 1845, John Louis O'Sullivan, a journalist, coined the phrase *Manifest Destiny*, a tenet holding that territorial expansion of the United States was not only inevitable but divinely ordained. Expansionist later used the phrase to justify acquisition of the territories west of the Mississippi. This, and the discovery of gold in California in 1849, opened a floodgate of migration into the territories that would forever change the west and its occupants.

Many the naive, young daydreamer saw visions of powered steamboats on coursing rivers and guided wagon trains taking them to their own destiny into the untamed wilderness and the riches beyond. Blind to the dangers, these adventurers set out on their journeys by any mode possible--on foot, horseback, mule or oxen drawn wagons, handcarts, rafts or canoes on rivers that happened to be going their way. All manner of individuals from different societies met and mingled on the trail. The weak among them would turn back or go insane before journey's end after "seeing the elephant," a euphemism for the horrors experienced on the trail.

Naive beginnings often led to tragedy but it was an education for most. The struggles on the trail forged a firm resolve that most often led to noble ends, but, in too many cases, to wretched depravation.

It has been said that the west was made up of the hardcore survivors. Rugged, trail-worn men and women, influenced by their Christian-Judao ideals, worked to carve a society out of the wilderness and to bring the territories into the Union.

And many among them were children.

OHIO

CINCINNATI

NEGROES ESCAPE

JOHNNY LEARNS ABOUT STEAMBOATS AND IRISH EMIGRANTS

OHIO R.

JOHNNY IS ENSLAVED

OHIO

THE MARY LANE DOCKED

PITTSBURGH

RAPIDS

ALLEGHENY

MONONGAHELA

PENNSYLVANIA

N

FORESTS OF THE UPPER ALLEGHENY

MILES

Chapter One

THE LORDS OF FATE

He left his young friend waving and shouting farewell from the snow-covered bank of the Allegheny River at Cornplanter while he maneuvered his raft through the fragmented ice out into the flow, heading south toward French Creek, bound for Pittsburgh. It was early April in the year 1852.

The icy waters of the Allegheny slipped by as the raft picked up speed. Johnny Farrell, having been taught by his father the Lead Raftsman for the Northern Forest Lumber Company, poled the raft skillfully past ice chunks, keeping it on course.

Coming into calmer waters where the river widened, Johnny sat down and removed a section of smoked venison ribs from his pack. He savored the rich, wild taste.

Johnny looked at the venison he held in his fingers. He had killed the deer a month before. His father praised Johnny for his skill with the muzzle loader before hanging the fresh kill in the smoke house. Remembering, a feeling of melancholy and loneliness settled over Johnny like a cold blanket. He pulled his heavy coat around him and began to reflect on the last days at Cornplanter. It was just a week before that Johnny had stood weeping over his father's grave in the cold cemetery on the hill. Father Slattery had just delivered the last prayers and the casket was being lowered. The priest came over, placed his hand on Johnny's shoulder and took him to the side.

"Joseph Schill is excited about your coming to live with him, Johnny," he said. "You are fortunate to have such fine folks willing to take you in."

"I know, Father. I know, but I have a destiny to fulfill. You know that. I have told you so," Johnny said.

"Foolish talk and a foolish destiny, Johnny," Father Slattery said. "I was hoping you had forgotten about such nonsense in light of your father's death."

"'Tis a dream, Father."

"Dreams are forgotten sooner than later."

Johnny sensed the priest's agitation. "Not my dream, Father."

"Son, you don't know of the world outside Cornplanter and Vogelbacher Settlement. You don't know of the wickedness. You know only good folks like the Schills and Vogelbachers. Folks who are willing to take you in as family."

Johnny felt a familiar anger rising within him. "I know that, Father. It's just that I am not ready for farmin'. Not yet. I want to see how other folks live. I want adventure, to see this country. I want to feel the weight of a nugget of gold in my hand. See the glitter of it lying upon the ground or shining up at me from the bottom of a riverbed."

"Son," Father Slattery said, "I fear what you will discover is the vileness of the world and it will harden your heart. When you no longer recognize it for what it is, you will have become part of it. I fear for your soul."

Johnny took a deep breath. "With all due respect, Father, I am strong in the Catholic Faith you have taught me. I just don't want it to confine me to this small world."

Father Slattery's hand fell from Johnny's shoulder. "Yours is a bright mind to be wasted on foolishness. We will talk again soon," he said.

Johnny watched as the priest mounted his horse. He turned, raised his right hand, blessed Johnny with the Sign of the Cross, then rode away. Johnny brushed off the remark about the wickedness of the world as just the ranting of a priest losing control of his pupil, but he also knew the subject wasn't finished as far as Father Slattery was concerned.

"C'mon Johnny," Joseph Schill said as he watched the priest ride south towards Vogelbacher Settlement. "Pa says you're to stay with us now. You got no other family. Someday you could be a raftsman like your pa was, but for now we need you to help us on the farm. Pa will be bringin' the wagon along for us in a couple days. Let's get your belongin's."

Johnny wasn't a tall boy but he was muscular for the age of sixteen. Ruddy-faced with auburn hair to the nape of his neck, his was the look of innocent youth; unworldly; unsophisticated.

Johnny's blue eyes usually smiled with a gleam of honesty, but today they were clouded with tears as he and his friend walked away from the grave toward the river.

"Pa hoped I would make better of myself someday," Johnny told his young friend, "Though he never did say in doin' what. He once told me, ''tis best to find the work you like first off 'cause it'll likely be the work yer stuck with the rest of yer life. A fellow has a way o' gettin' stuck inna rut owin' this one and that,' he'd say."

Joseph, a brown eyed sandy complected boy with brown hair, the son of German immigrants, was excited with the prospects of Johnny living with them. Being twelve, and the oldest boy of his family, he looked upon Johnny as one would an admired older brother.

"There's nothin' else doin' in Cornplanter 'cept fetchin' buckets of surface oil up the creek," Joseph reasoned. "Raftin' pays good and it's steady work most of the year. But farmin' at Vogelbacher Settlement, now there's a trade for a lifetime, I say."

The two boys stopped on a bluff overlooking the river. Johnny's eye caught a piece of ice disappearing around the bend where the river turned south. He thought of the many times as a younger boy how often he wondered about the journey those chunks of ice were taking, and what they encountered along the way.

"You and your ma and pa are mighty fine folks, Joseph," Johnny said as he gazed down the river, "and I don't mind farmin', but I know your folks are going to expect me to take schoolin' during the winter months until plowing and planting time in the spring. I just can't abide the thoughts of sitting in a classroom any longer. Truth be told, Joseph, I've got the adventuresome spirit. I want to raft down that river. I gotta see the other end of that river and whatever is beyond. Pa once told me you can go all the way to the frontier by river boat, all the way to Missouri."

"An' what would you do in Missouri, Johnny?" Joseph argued.

"I wouldn't stop there, Joseph. I'd keep on goin' west. Word has it there is gold just layin' on the ground out there, waitin' to be picked up."

"Ya mean like the oil lays atop the ground here?" Joseph grumbled as he jumped over a puddle of oil slick mud.

"Sure," Johnny agreed.

"Well, how would you get down river, Johnny, you got no raft."

"Sure do," Johnny said, "See it out there on the river."

Joseph looked toward the river, but saw nothing resembling a raft.

"Huh!" he exclaimed, his eyes still searching the river.

"You see those logs?" Johnny asked, pointing at a number of logs trapped by ice near the bank, some of the cargo from his father's ill-fated rafts. "I'm thinkin' there're some hardwood logs in those shallows. Pa showed me how to make a raft. I can build one just big enough to ride the rapids and small enough to pole by myself."

"I dunno Johnny," Joseph worried. "I hear there are some mighty rough rapids south of French Creek and rocks and sand bars and . . ."

Johnny stopped him short. "I know, Joseph, but I'm not scared. I don't think about it. It's a sure thing though, I've got to do it before the spring rains melt the snow an' breaks all that ice free. C'mon, help me build a raft. We'll need some rawhide to cut into straps and some hide so I can make a shelter. Pa has a deer hide drying out back, go fetch it while I wrestle some of those logs ashore."

A few days later, the raft floated at the river's icy edge moored to a tree its twelve foot logs secured with rawhide and nails. In the center of the raft was a small deerskin tent fashioned in the style of a tepee. Johnny placed his blankets inside the tent along with some smoked venison ribs, salt pork, and a jug of fresh spring water. He pulled his fleece coat about his ears to ward off the cold.

"It's sure a fine lookin' raft, Joseph. Pa told me to use rawhide on the logs 'cause the raft would ride the rapids better."

"Johnny, I sure wish I could talk you outta this," Joseph worried. "I was lookin' for you to be coming to live with us. If my pa knew what you were up to he'd put a stop to it. I'll for sure catch it when he gets here and you're gone."

"Yer a good friend, Joseph. I'll remember you everywhere I go," Johnny said.

"This week has been sorrowful enough with yer pa gettin' killed raftin' those logs. Now you're preparin' to follow him with this fool contrivance," Joseph shot back, pointing at the newly constructed raft.

"Partin's always sad for me, Joseph. Funny thing though, I feel sad and excited all at the same time. I look at that river and I sometimes feel like it's gonna swallow me up and at other times I feel like it's gonna take me to my dreams fulfillment."

"Most likely swallow you up," Joseph retorted.

Johnny loaded the rest of the supplies on the raft.

"Look now," Joseph continued, "I went along with building this raft 'cause it was fun, and it took your mind off your pa's passin'. I really never thought you were serious about raftin' that dang river. If you get hurt, or worse yet drowned, I'll feel like I had a hand in it."

"Throw me that rope there, Joseph." Joseph picked up the rope and handed it to Johnny.

"Don't worry about me,"Johnny continued. "It's the Lord's will whatever happens. He'll not let guilt rest upon your head. Tell your pa I know what I'm doin'. Tell him I'll be forever indebted to his kind offer and I'll try to be back next spring to help him with the plantin'. Tell Father Slattery I shall miss him and I will carry the faith he taught me close to my heart. It will forever be my guidance."

Standing on the raft with pole in hand, Johnny saw tears welling up in Joseph's brown eyes. "Untie my line there, Joseph. Don't cry now. I'll be fine. When I come back, we'll go huntin' again. You gotta practice loadin' your pa's rifle. I know it's heavy for ya but you'll get the hang of it. Do it like I showed ya."

"Wait Johnny, I want you to have this." Sniffling, Joseph removed the hunting knife and scabbard from his belt.

"Joseph! Are you sure? That's the bone handled knife your pa made for you."

"Yeah, somethin' to remember me by and protect yourself with. Luck to you, Johnny. Mind you now, the Lords of Fate." Joseph untied the mooring rope and threw it on board.

Johnny threaded the knife and scabbard in his belt.

Memories of nightmares about the Lords of Fate flooded his mind. Those devilish characters who waited in the wings of his worst dreams, threatening to carry him to his death. His imagery had invented white knights as protectors. After bad dreams Johnny would tell Joseph about the Lords of Fate and how the Knights of Goodness would save him. Though now, he wished Joseph had not brought up the subject.

Johnny pushed his long pole into the river bank and shoved off. "Take care, Joseph. The Lords of Fate be hanged. I shall call upon the Knights of Goodness for protection, and be back soon's I get rich."

Slowly Johnny guided the raft out to catch the current where it picked up the speed of the flow. Johnny looked back and saw Joseph waving from the bank. His figure grew smaller and finally disappeared as the raft made the turn in the river toward the south.

Alone on his raft, Johnny smiled through misty eyes thinking about Joseph. He threw the last of the bony remains of the venison ribs into the water, wiping his hands on his trousers. He took up the pole to guide his raft. Suddenly he faced an awesome sight of high rock outcroppings in a mountain gorge. He let the raft drift with the current and admired the passing cliffs.

The distant sounds of fierce growling and an animal in distress drew Johnny's attention to an outcropping of rock at the top of the cliff on the east side of the river. An old bull elk was making a desperate stand against a pack of wolves.

One of the wolves charged from the front to distract the elk while two others tried to move in from behind. The elk backed up closer to the edge of the outcropping to protect his flank. He jabbed at the rushing wolf with his foreleg and caught him in the chest, rolling the wolf over. One of the wolves came in from the rear with teeth bared and growling. The elk kicked swiftly with his hind leg, caught the wolf squarely on his underbelly lifting, him several feet into the air and over the edge.

Johnny watched as the wolf wiggled and flopped trying to right itself while it fell down the side of the cliff and yelped as it met its death on the jagged rocks below.

Johnny's attention was drawn back to the struggle at the top of the cliff with the sound of wolves growling and barking and the elk screaming with each savage attack. The wolves, salivating, buried their fangs deep into the elks muscle, tearing and ripping him open. Blood streamed out of gaping wounds and matted his fur. Instinctively and with fury the elk fought on until, weakened and weary from exhaustion and loss of blood, he was pulled to the ground.

Johnny could see no more, but knew it was over. He accepted the struggle as part of nature in the wilderness and felt reassured that mankind was above such violence, survival being less dramatic for humans.

The river grew narrow and deep in this gaping mountain gorge, the pole no longer reached the bottom. Johnny continued to drift with the current. He used the pole only to keep away from the crags along the bank. Blocked by the high walls of the ravine, the sun was almost straight overhead before it cast its warming rays upon the raft. Soon after, the sun disappeared behind the west wall, the river widened and the rocky cliffs gave way to rolling mountains of oak, maple and laurel not yet in foliage.

Johnny noticed, off to the southwest, a dark storm cloud. A warm breeze started blowing in from that direction.

"That ain't no snow cloud, looks like rain," he said. Dejected, he thought of the sudden changes in temperature that sometimes occurred in April in the Allegheny mountains and of what a quick thaw meant in the Allegheny watershed.

In a short period of time the sky above him began to darken and the wind picked up. Johnny scanned the river bank for a place to tie off and wait out the storm.

Darkness had set in by the time he found a clearing in the ice that would allow him near enough to the river bank to secure his raft to a tree. After a supper of smoked venison and spring water, he crawled into his tent and wrapped himself in fur blankets.

The rain started at first with a few loud taps on the rawhide tent. Then more droplets, beating faster. Soon the heavens opened and the rain hammered at the tent roof.

Johnny listened to the rhythmic beat until it, and the rocking and pitching of the raft in the water, lulled him to sleep.

Morning came quickly and Johnny, expecting to hear the rain that put him to sleep, awoke to silence. He propped himself on his elbows, his ears perked to hear a sound. The river no longer rocked the raft under him. Then he sensed calm but fast motion. Throwing his blankets off Johnny scrambled out of the tent. The warm rains of the night before had melted the snow and broke all ice jams for miles upriver. Through low hanging fog he saw a fast moving, swollen river. Moving like ghostly figures, large fragments of ice appeared out of the fog and slowly disappeared again.

Johnny felt a sharp twinge of fear shoot from his belly to his throat. He whirled around in search of his pole to push away from any ice that might threaten his raft. It was gone! Then he discovered the mooring line and several of the forward logs were gone. His rawhide lacing was coming undone. His raft was slowly coming apart. Squinting through the fog he looked for the ice fragments he knew were out there somewhere moving in closer. The thought of his situation began to anger him. "The Lords of Fate have come to get me," he said.

"Well," he hollered raising his fists over his head, "you ain't gonna get me yet. Not today, I ain't ready to die. You think I ain't got nothin' to say about this? You just watch . . ."

Johnny's words froze in his mouth. To his left, moving with him, a massive segment of ice emerged out of the fog. On his hands and knees now, Johnny strained his eyes through the fog to his right for another sizable chunk, not wanting to be caught between them or against a rocky shore line. He listened intently and watched for sound or sight of impending disaster. He could feel the raft pick up speed as it raised and lowered over whispering waves. His body tensed. Fear tied a knot in his throat. Sweat broke over his brow though the fog was cold and wet.

Suddenly, appearing out of the fog like a monster out of the deep, large slabs of ice, piled up against one another, protruded into the air.

The raft rode vertically up the ice, separating logs from rawhide, throwing Johnny into the frigid water. His heavy fleece coat pulled him under. As he struggled to remove the coat, his lungs began to hurt for air. Free of the coat now Johnny tried to surface, but found himself under the ice. He strained his eyes through the muddy water, looking for light indicating a clearing. He felt his lungs ready to burst when his hands reached the edge of the ice above water. Pulling himself to the surface, coughing and choking, he groped around for something to grab. Several logs floated nearby, nudging the ice. Johnny pulled himself up on one, seized a second one and straddled them both. He lay there, taking deep breaths of precious fresh air, ridding his lungs of river water.

Johnny had no idea of the distance he had traveled during the night, but at the rate the river flowed, he suspected Pittsburgh should not be too far ahead.

In his struggle he hadn't had time to think of how cold and miserable he was. His legs and arms began to grow numb as he fought to maintain balance on the logs. "Got to hang on," he muttered.

At a distance in front of him he heard something vaguely familiar -- the sound of rushing water as if over a falls or. . . .

The thought froze in his mind and he was somewhat surprised by a noise that jumped from his throat. Like that of a whimpering dog. He pulled himself up on one of the logs, straining his eyes into the fog. The sound grew louder. It now seemed all around him. Just as he saw the white water he was upon it.

"Rapids!" he screamed.

Johnny grasped the logs and hung on with his numb hands and aching arms. He felt the surge as the logs approached the swift moving water of the rapids.

A round boulder of exceptional size projected into the river from the right. The water roared over the rock and down into an abyss. Helpless and at the whim of the water's flow, Johnny went over the top and straight down into the foaming recesses of the river's bowels; swallowed alive, it seemed, by a frothing giant.

Just as quickly, two logs lunged from the water and splashed to the surface. Astride them was Johnny, hugging the logs, gasping for air. The logs moved swiftly with the rushing water, dipping and rising around rocks and what were now broken, harmless pieces of ice. Johnny, now delirious from exposure, heard voices. "Give it up, boy, give up now. Just go to sleep. You be nice and warm if you do. Just like sittin' in front of a warm fire. All you got to do is go to sleep."

"The Lords of Fate," Johnny reasoned in spite of his misery. "Oh Knights of Goodness impale those evil lords upon thy swords of justice," he whispered.

With effort he raised his head. The fog was gone. The sun broke through clouds. Here and there he saw reflections glistening in the now calm waters. He was being drawn by the confluence of two rivers. To his left he could see far up the other river, but he and his logs were being drawn to the west. Now he saw buildings along the shore and large boats moored to wooden piers.

He laid his head back down. "Dern Lords of Fate playin' tricks on my eyes now."

Johnny began to feel warm all over. His eyes began to feel drowsy and he wanted to sleep. He was no longer aware of the logs or the lower part of his body.

"Come on boy, grab on. Take holt da rope. I'll help ya."

"Sure ya will, ya hated devil. You'd like ta help me straight inta hell, sure 'nuff," he yelled in anger as he raised his head.

In front of his face, a rope dangled. A loop on the end lay across the logs.

"Ya call me a hated devil agin an' see what ah do wit dis rope. Now, grab da damn rope, boy. Ah got better things ta do den fishin' fer da likes ah you. If ah haf ta come inta dat cold water ta git ya ah'll cut yer gizzard out and feed it ta da fish."

Johnny reached out for the rope and slowly placed the loop under his arms.

At that moment, the rope tightened around him. He felt himself being pulled up. An arm reached out for him. At the other end of that arm was the ugliest face he had ever seen.

The Lords of Fate have won. I see the face of Satan himself, he was thinking just before his body went limp.

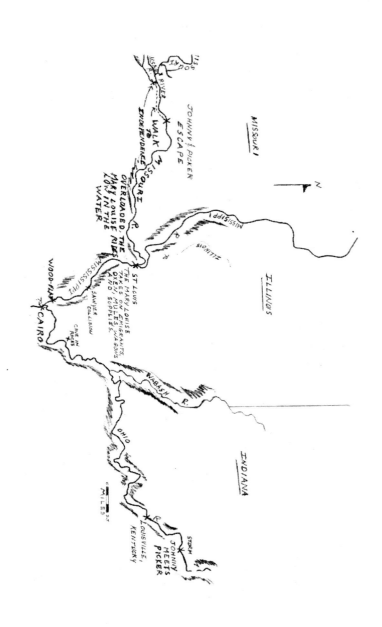

Chapter Two

THE MATE

"Hey boy, you hear me?" a man's voice questioned.

Johnny thought he heard a voice. It wasn't important. He was warm and dry and that was all that mattered. Just let me sleep, he thought.

"He ain't come 'round yet," the voice said. "Like to find out who he is and where his folks are so's we can cast off. Got a full head of steam ready to bust loose."

"Who's there?" Johnny asked, still half asleep.

"Names Pierce, Captain Tyler Pierce, son. How do you feel?"

Johnny opened his eyes and looked around a very strange room with varnished wood, like the wood that encircled his mother's cherished store-bought oval mirror. A stern, heavy man with a black beard and pipe stood over him with hands fisted on his hips.

"Where am I?" Johnny asked in a daze.

"You're in the captain's cabin 'board the steamboat Mary Louise," Captain Pierce answered. "Who are you and how did you come to be clingin' to a log floatin' down the Ohio River? We fished you out the forenoon two days back. You're lucky we saw you. Twern't much life left in you. Considered throwin' you back."

"Name's Johnny Farrell from Cornplanter on the Allegheny. I poled out from Cornplanter on a raft headed for Pittsburgh. Got caught unawares in a storm. My raft broke up. Don't remember much after that cept hangin' on fer life to a couple logs."

"You rafted the Allegheny by yourself in the midst of spring run off? You could have got yourself killed, lad. If not by the rapids, then surely by the ice flow. Why, I've seen ice chunks big as steamboats on that river. If we hadn't found you the way we did, I would not believe you."

"I can promise you, sir," Johnny assured him, "I don't believe I'll be doin' it agin any too soon."

"Well, you made it to Pittsburgh, son. Now I have to see you get back to your folks."

"I got no folks, sir," Johnny hastened. "My ma died when I was young and my pa was killed a week past. He was a master raftsman on the Allegheny."

"So that's how you learned to raft, huh," the captain concluded.

"Yes sir," Johnny said, "'though I'm not so sure Pa would have been proud to see me now, bein' as how you had to fish me out."

"You did your pa proud, lad," the captain assured him. "You're a brave boy."

"Yeah, but Pa always said, 'a cup a common sense is worth more'an a jug a derrin'-do'," Johnny admitted.

"Your pa must have been a wise man," the captain said, "but now what will you do, son? I must be casting off for points west. We have a head a steam up and the pilot is getting impatient."

"Take me with you, sir," Johnny asked, "It's the frontier I'm off to. I got money." Johnny reached into his pocket but found it empty, then he noticed his knife was gone from his scabbard.

"Hey, where's my money and my bone handled knife?"

"Must have lost it in the river," the captain assured him, "the way you are, is the way they brought you in here? You almost lost yer britches when they pulled you outta the water."

"I'll work my way, sir," Johnny insisted. "I'm strong. I can do anything."

"Well," the captain said, rubbing his beard, "I can't seem to keep a full crew of roustabouts. Seems I lose one at almost every port. I'm sure the first mate could use another. We off load lumber at Westport Landing in Missouri, if it's the frontier you want. The wagon trains form up at Independence three miles south of there."

"I'll do it," Johnny insisted, not knowing what a roustabout was or what his duties aboard a steamboat might be.

"The clerk will pay your wages upon arrival in Westport. Once in Westport you're no longer my responsibility. You're on your own," the Captain instructed.

"Fair 'nuff," Johnny said, "and thanks much, sir."

"I'm not sure you want to be thanking me, boy," the captain said warily. "Go tell the mate you're hired on, but don't tell him you're Irish. The mate doesn't like Irish so much."

"Who might the mate be, sir?" Johnny asked.

"You will know him when you see him, son. He's the one who fished you out of the river. Good luck to you."

Johnny suddenly had an ominous feeling about his situation but wasn't sure why. He couldn't remember being fished out of the river. He climbed down the ladder from the captain's cabin and quickly realized the enormity of the boat. Until now all he had ever seen on water were rafts and flatboats on the Allegheny.

On both sides of the deck were huge paddle wheels being driven, he had been told, by steam engines somewhere in the belly of the boat. Setting side by side and towards the bow, two towering, fluted, stacks bilging smoke rose just above the glass-walled square pilot house. Milled lumber from the forest of the northern Allegheny was stacked neatly on the lower decks just aft of the paddle wheels. Johnny paused by the lumber and thought of the many loads of logs his pa had rafted down the Allegheny to the mills in Pittsburgh in the years before he was killed. He wondered if the lumber would be used to build homes on the newly settled frontier. The thought of the frontier and the wilderness beyond excited him. He became aware of his good fortune, being aboard the *Mary Louise*.

"Lords of Fate, hah! I stand victorious!"

Suddenly, he sensed the presence of someone. He turned and was startled by a ghastly face. He quickly surmised it was the mate.

He had a patch over his right eye, a missing front tooth and numerous scars. One of the scars protruded from the patch and curved down the side of his face to the corner of his mouth, distorting that portion of his expression into a hideous grimace. A pistol was lodged in his waste belt. Hanging beside the pistol, Johnny recognized his bone handled knife.

The mate stood before Johnny with his fist pressed against his hips, feet parted. "What's yar bizniz on da decks, boy?"

"The captin, ah, Captin Pierce, sir, he said I was to report to you, sir. He hired me on as a roustabout."

"Ya 'er been a roustabout afore?" the mate asked with growing impatience.

"No sir, I don't even know whatta roustabout is," Johnny replied nervously, sensing the mate's impatience.

"Well, lemme give ya an idea," the mate shot back, "so's ya have no doubt were ya stand 'round here. The captin' dere, he in charge, somewhat, but the pilot runs the boat. The engineer keeps the engines runnin' when he's sober. The clerk takes care ah the books, and the mate in charge ah the roustabouts, the lowest humans on dis boat, if ya can call 'em human."

"Yes, sir," Johnny said. "Aaah, I see you found my knife. I thought I lost it in the riv . . ."

The mate grabbed Johnny by the neck and backed him into a corner behind a stack of lumber out of site of the passenger deck and the captain's cabin. In a flash, he pulled the knife from his belt and pressed the point against Johnny's throat. Johnny was frightened and wanted to swallow but was afraid the motion would puncture his throat. "What 'er ya doin'?" Johnny half whispered in panic.

"Ya 'err stick a man, scum?"

"N-N-No," Johnny stammered.

"Thar's nothin' to it," the mate said.

"I cuts a man's stomach open when I kills 'em," the mate moved the knife from Johnny's throat down to the bottom of his rib cage. "I cuts him fr'm here," he moved the knife blade down below his belly button and stopped, "ta here, and yanks 'is entrails out afore I throws 'em overboard. Dat's so's he sinks to da bottom and don' float fer someone ta find 'is body."

Johnny felt his stomach churn.

The mate pulled back and put the knife back in his belt. "And sometimes I jest take sport in kickin' and gougin' roustabouts for the fun ah it. Now git below." The mate unlocked a trap door leading to a hold below deck.

"I keeps law and order on dis boat wit me barrel stave. If ya don wanna feel it 'cross yar skull, ya'll do as yar tolt."

Johnny hastened down a ladder into the dim glow of candle light in the hold. A stench choked him as he descended. Reaching the bottom, he found himself in the middle of a half dozen or so unwashed, malnourished men. Some were sitting on the sodden planks of the floor, laying against the haul. All appeared weary and tired and looked straight ahead with hollow stares.

"Well laddy, what be ye'r name now?" one of them asked.

"Johnny Farrell," he answered hesitantly, looking around trying to comprehend what his eyes were seeing.

"Farrell. Ah yes, a good Irish name, but ye'll not be from Ireland. Where might 'ee be from, may I ask?"

"Cornplanter on the Allegheny," Johnny replied as he gazed upon this group of strange men.

The Irishman looked puzzled.

"The Allegheny is a river in Pennsylvania," Johnny explained. Then asked, "How long have you been on this boat?"

"Awe laddy, we lost track've time long ago. Time has little meaning for us," he replied sadly.

"I don't understand," Johnny challenged.

The Irishman laughed bitterly. "Laddy, we left home in bonny Ireland hopin' t' find a better life in America.

We found hatred instead. We have t' survive as best we can on our own or perish. On this boat, at least, we eat. Tha' tis, we eat wha' the class passengers on the top deck ·leave over."

"You mean," Johnny grimaced, "their garbage?"

"Well now lad, that's all 'n how ye're lookin' at it."

"What wages do they pay you?" Johnny asked, anticipating the answer.

Again the Irishman laughed bitterly and shrugged his shoulders in defeat.

Johnny looked at the Irishman and, not getting an answer, said, "Ya don't git pay for yer work?" Johnny thought for a few seconds, "Yer slaves then!" he said.

"No laddy, the Negroes in the other hold are slaves. They're fed well n' treated better because they're bought and paid for. They're valuable property. They did not chose t'come to this country. They were brought here at great expense. The Irishman, on the other hand, came o'er of 'is own free will by the droves. Because there are so many of us we're reviled and thought of as expendable. We're worked to exhaustion and when we cannot work any longer, or get too sick to work, we are thrown overboard. Those who're able to swim, try to, but very few survive. When we come into the northern free states, the Negroes are made to stay below outtov sight and we are used as white labor to load and unload cargo."

Johnny leaned against the haul and slid down to sit with his elbows on his knees, as did the other roustabouts. His mind was trying to grasp all that he was hearing and seeing. Perplexed, he muttered, "Why do men treat other men like that?"

"Dunno for sure, laddy," the Irishman shrugged, "but I suspect it has to do with power and prejudice. One man's power over 'nother or race over 'nother and who happens to be holdin' the power at the time. The power of the majority, or those with the money, or maybe ignorance. Power and ignorance, 'tis a dangerous mixture."

"Not sure I understand yer meanin'," Johnny puzzled.

"Sounds like you had some schoolin' in yer day."

"Oh, some. Mostly I learned from livin', just as you will lad."

"I've learned a lot at my mother's knee and from pa and Father Slattery, my confessor," Johnny assured him, "but there's still lots to learn 'bout life, I'm thinkin'. Well, I'm off this boat in Westport Landing, Missouri." Johnny tried to cheer himself up. "Gonna head west to the gold fields of California."

"That's a mighty fine dream, laddy. Dreams keep us alive. 'Tis good to have a dream. We all have dreams down here, but we got no hope."

"Mine ain't no dream," Johnny shot back, "it's a fact."

"Sure, laddy. Fact is, you'll no be seein' Westport Landing for long," the Irishman assured him.

"Whatta ya mean," Johnny demanded, "the captin said I'd be on this boat as far as Westport Landing."

"Yes, and I'm sure he has already advised the mate of that, but, the captin doesn't know what goes down here, he never leaves the passenger deck. The mate doesn't intend to let you leave this boat, laddy. At least not until he's finished with you. He has a use for you or he wouldn't have fished 'ee out of the river I'm guessin'. He would have let 'ee drown. No laddy, I'm afraid ye'er one of us now."

Chapter Three

LEARNING NEW THINGS

Rolling and tossing on the uneven planks of the boat's hold floor, sleep was becoming as elusive as freedom for Johnny. The waters of the Ohio, flowing around the prow, made a trickling sound inside the hull. Johnny's mind wondered to Cornplanter on the Allegheny and the clear running streams and brooks, cascading down heavily wooded mountains to the river. In his mind's eye he could see a deer standing at the river's edge, water dripping from its mouth, having quickly raised its head to the sound, or maybe the scent, of something far off. It turns and takes two cautious steps toward a stand of willows, looks back, then vanishes into the green. What grace, Johnny thought, so free. So clean and fresh the air.

Johnny's eyes opened wide to the darkness and stench of the hold. He pulled himself up on his elbows. He must escape. But how? "No man has ever escaped before, not alive anyhow," the Irishman had said, "The mate enjoys torturing and killing those who try."

Johnny shuddered at the thought, but knew he had to get off this boat. I am of a free spirit and my destiny lies in the open country of the frontier. He reminded himself of what his father had once told him when faced with, what seemed at the time, an impossible situation.

"Son, if ya intend ta take the rabbit from the wolves mouth, ya better be a lot smarter than he an' a damn sight hungrier 'cause surin's hell he ain't gonna give it ta ya outta kindness."

Johnny heard footsteps on the deck above.

"That be the mate, laddy," the Irishman whispered. "He's comin' to lock down the hatch. Every night at the same time we hear his footsteps to the hatch cover, then, the sound of the lock against the hatch, 'clack', then the sound of the lock closing, 'click'. Clack, click every night, clack, click."

Johnny waited to hear the hatch being locked. The footsteps stopped at the hatch cover, hesitated, then continued on.

Johnny sat up quickly. "He didn't lock it," he whispered anxiously.

"Nay, laddy," the Irishman laid a firm hand on Johnny's shoulder. "One night one of the roustabouts figured the mate forgot to lock the hatch and the poor fool tried to make good an escape. The mate was waiting for 'im, for all we heard was a muffled scream and a splash in the water. We are wise to him now. No one tries to escape n' more."

"Yeah," Johnny said, brushing the hand from his shoulder, "but that poor feller didn't know the mate was waitin' for him. There's no moon tonight. I'll wait 'til the deck lanterns are turned down then crawl along the decking in the shadows of the stacked lumber and . . ."

"Nay, laddy," the Irishman interrupted, "the mate is baitin' us. Mind ya now he would toy with 'ee like a cat with a mouse. You would only get as far as he let 'ee beyond that hatch door. He is watchin', lad, believe it."

Johnny laid back down on the hard planks. "Capt'n Pierce promised to pay my wages when we arrive in Westport Landing," he said in despair.

"Oh, he will that laddy. Tha' tis, he'll instruct the purser to pay yeer wages, but, the purser and the mate will divide yeer wages amongst themselves."

"Well then," Johnny exclaimed, "I'll just tell the capt'n about this. He seemed a fair enough man."

Johnny heard muffled laughter from other men.

"An' just how do ee plan to talk to the captain, laddy?" the Irishman responded, "that requires permission from the mate. The captain never comes down to the lower decks. He's always on the upper deck with the passengers or in his quarters. The mate never gives permission to talk to the captain for any reason. That way the captain thinks all hands are happy." He added gesturing with his hand, "no complaints."

"Well," Johnny concluded, "I won't try to escape tonight."

"Ah good now, laddy, best ye not make trouble, lest we all get short rations on the morrow." The Irishman relaxed.

"Instead," Johnny continued, "I'll make my way to the captain's quarters and let him know all is not right aboard his boat."

Out of the corner of his eye Johnny thought he saw the Irishman throw up his hands.

"Who's to say fer sure we're goin' to Missouri?" Johnny asked. "We may be goin' back to Louisiana. Then how would I get to the frontier?"

"I never know where we go, laddy, but me guess is the lumber we just loaded in Pittsburgh's on its way to the frontier. If that be so we will steam down the Ohio River to the Mississippi river, then up the Mississippi to the Missouri river. Be 'bout six days if we don't run into heavy storms n' head winds."

Six days, Johnny thought, six days if that's where we're goin'.

Johnny lay for hours after the candles were extinguished, listening to the gurgling of the river against the hull and the occasional grunt or snore of the hold occupants.

When he sensed the time was right, he raised slowly to his feet. Taking care not to disturb the Irishman, he felt along the hull planking for the ladder leading to the hatch. He climbed the ladder and gently lifted the hatch cover which opened to the stern.

The deck lanterns had been shut down except for one on the main passenger deck that shown a faint light down on the cargo deck where Johnny had emerged.

The quiet of the night was disturbed only by the song of a whippoorwill from a distance on shore. Gradually Johnny lifted and moved the hatch cover over just far enough to crawl out. He lay flat on the deck, taking in the situation around him.

The milled lumber, stacked at mid-deck for balance, was between him and the ladder to the passenger's deck and captain's cabin. Though the mate was nowhere in sight, he belly-crawled to the stacks of lumber. Once there, he stood with his back against the lumber. He then crept to the corner of the stack and peered around it.

The sweet smell of the fresh milled lumber lingered on Johnny's senses, but was quickly replaced by the sour smell of sweat as an arm came around his neck and cut off his breathing. "Gotcha," a throaty voice rasped.

A cold knife point pricked him just below the rib cage. He was lifted off his feet to the tips of his toes. "Har, it's da new boy," the mate whispered as he dragged Johnny back into the shadows of the lumber on the larboard side.

"Where ya be off ta now? Ya have a dinner engagement wit da captin do ya? Ah'll let 'em know you be otterwise engaged an' he will not have da honor of yer presence."

Johnny was getting dizzy with fear and lack of air. He waited for the thrust of the knife into his heart, the knife Joseph had given him.

"Ah'd like ta cut yer throat and throw ya overboard like ah did da last one, but, it seems da last one was da stoker. Now da engineer is mad 'cause his stoker dis'peared an' he been doin his own stokin', but, da engineer gonna be happy agin cause you gonna be his stoker. Har, after stokin' da furnace all day you be too tired ta think 'bout goin' ta dinner parties in da ev'nin'."

Standing over the hold now the mate kicked the cover aside. Lifting Johnny off the deck, he dropped him into the hold.

The Irishman, having been awakened by the commotion and drawn to the hold ladder to investigate, broke Johnny's fall and both went crashing to the hold floor.

The mate replaced the hatch cover and locked it down.

"The mate has had 'is fun this night," the Irishman said as he helped Johnny to a sitting position, "and you, laddy, are a very lucky Irish boy indeed."

* * * * *

The days steaming down the Ohio were quiet and un-eventful, except for Johnny's new duty of stoking the boiler furnace. The heat in the furnace area brought him to the edge of exhaustion and sleep at night, even on the planks of the hold floor, came easy.

He had seen a steamer once on the Allegheny and had heard his father talk of them and was in wonder of how they worked. The engineer to whom he was as-signed, explained the importance of keeping the fire in the furnace at a certain level to maintain a boiling point of the water in the boiler. "That," he said, "is all you need to know."

Johnny's inquisitive nature, however, soon had the engineer explaining more and more. He came to under-stand the relationship between the amount of fuel, the water temperature, and the amount of steam pressure. He was also sternly advised of the possible results if this relationship was not maintained properly, that is, the boiler would blow up and the entire vessel along with it.

"Many the steamboat have gone to the bottom, what's left of them anyway," he told Johnny, "because an engineer got drunk and didn't mind the business at hand." Pointing toward the front of the boiler above the furnace the engineer continued, "Ya see that lever and gauge there? That's the pressure gauge and lever safety valve."

Johnny's attention was drawn to the gauge and lever above the furnace. They were attached to a pipe from the boiler by a coupling on both sides.

The engineer went on, "If the pressure of the steam goes above this level," he said, pointing at the gauge on the meter, "ya pull the lever to release the pressure if it hadn't already been released to the pistons. Of course it would not be released to the pistons if we were settin' at dockside. We now got one of these newfangled automatic pressure release valves," he said, pointing above the metered gauge to a strange looking device mounted with couplings around and bypassing the release arm to the pipe running up the stacks. "I don't trust the contraption. I don't trust my life to nothin' I can do better myself . . ."

The engineer proceeded with his detailed explanation, but Johnny's mind was fixed on the release arm, the gauge, and the coupling to the pipe which ran along the smoke stack.

"...the steam would then exit safely high above the hurricane deck and pilothouse," the engineer concluded.

Early the next morning while Johnny pitched more coal into the furnaces in preparation for departure, his mind was feverishly working on a way he could use his new-found knowledge to perfect an escape plan. The door of the furnace was opened wide like a hungry monster gulping up the coal Johnny tossed in as fast as he could shovel it. Engrossed in deep concentration he did not heed the furnace as it began to roar. The pointer on the pressure gauge climbed. He stopped shoveling to catch his breath. Leaning on the shovel, he stared into the pile of coal.

Outside, above the pilothouse the stacks belched black smoke that drew the attention of every hand on deck, including the mate and engineer.

Think, he thought to himself, think. The gauge, the release lever, steam pressure. There must be a wa . . .

"Pressure!" he shouted. Turning his head in the direction of the gauge, Johnny's eyes fixed on the position of the pointer. He froze for a moment than ran to the release lever, but just as he pulled the lever the automatic valve operated. Steam was released in both directions. At that moment the engineer and mate burst into the furnace room and ran toward the boiler. The engineer frantically reached for the release lever, finding it already released.

High above the hurricane deck the steam hissed and roared up through the black plume of smoke that floated on a gentle breeze down river. All those passengers who had not yet awakened were pulled abruptly into the dawn of a new day.

"Fool," the mate yelled as he smashed Johnny across the mouth with a swinging back hand that sent him stumbling and falling in a heap in the corner.

The engineer, shaken and angry, called into the speaking tube that connected the engine room to the pilothouse, "Steams up,"

A muffled voice from the pilothouse and the sound of bells indicated they should get underway. The engineer engaged the steam pistons and the side wheels began to rumble and thrash.

As Johnny wiped his sleeve across his bleeding mouth, the engineer shot a glaring look in his direction and shook his head.

"I-I'm sorry," Johnny stammered as he realized what had almost happened.

"Sorry?" the engineer retorted. "Ya dang near blew us into the next county an' all you got to say is you're 'sorry'? At least ya had the since to pull the release lever."

"I think I understand 'bout pressure and such things now," Johnny said, pulling himself from the floor, "I'll know better next time. I swear, it won't happen again. The auto . . ."

Just as Johnny was about to tell the engineer about the automatic valve having worked properly, the mate pulled his knife from his belt. He grabbed Johnny by the hair, pulling his head backwards, forcing him to his knees, exposing his throat.

The mate drew his blade back ready to thrust. "Dere ain't gonna be a next time for you, scum."

"Wait," the engineer stepped over holding back the mate's arm. "I don't want his blood all over the engine room floor an' damn it, I want you to quit cuttin' my stokers. He works for me and I'll decide his punishment. I don't believe he'll be forgettin' how close he came to meetin' his maker this day. He'll pay 'tention from now on, I'm sure. Isn't that right, lad?"

"Y-Yes, sir," Johnny stammered as the mate kicked him to the floor.

The fear of his close encounter with death brushed away all thoughts of the automatic release valve. The only conscious thought he had was that of getting off this boat as quickly as possible before the mate killed him for sure.

Johnny's work day ended and he moved off toward the hold door holding his ribs where he had been kicked. A movement on the passenger deck above caught his attention. Looking up he observed a very pretty young girl not more than 16 years, he guessed. She wore a long full cotton dress to the ankles with sleeves ruffled at the wrist. A hooded shawl draped her bodice and covered her head. Curls fell from the hood and cascaded over her shoulders. She looked in Johnny's direction and met his eyes and a smile creased her face. Johnny felt a strange tingling in his body and almost raised his hand to wave before she turned and walked away.

Frozen for a moment in a strange world of feelings, Johnny forgot his pained ribs and returned to the hold for the night.

In the darkness of the hold he wanted to ask the Irishman about the feelings, but wasn't sure how to go about that. Finally he just blurted it out. "Have you ever...? Aaaah, well, I got these feelin's." Johnny stammered over the words.

"Are ye all right, lad? Ye have a fever or somethin'? Lord Almighty ye don't 'ave the cholera do ye?"

"Cholera? What does cholera feel like?" Johnny puzzled over the question.

"It starts with the sickness in the stomach and the chills," the Irishman explained.

"No, I don't think I have cholera unless you can get it from lookin' at a pretty girl."

"What!" rose out of the darkness.

"Well, I guess I did more than just look," Johnny tried to be honest, feeling a little bit guilty for his thoughts.

"You did what?" A pause, then, "With who, laddy?"

"A pretty girl on the passenger deck," Johnny explained a little embarrassed despite the darkness.

"Ye was up on the passenger deck, laddy?"

"No, down by the lumber stack."

"Ye had her down by the lumber stack?"

"No, she was on the passenger deck."

There was silence in the darkness for a moment, then, "What exactly did ye do with this pretty girl, laddy?"

"Nothin," Johnny answered.

"Ye wouldn't lie t'me now would ye lad? Ye said ye did more than look. What 'more' did ye do, huh?"

"I guess it's more in what she did," Johnny wondered where all this was going and wished he hadn't started it.

"What she did?" came the retort, "What did she do?"

"She smiled at me," Johnny replied.

There was a silence for a moment, then laughter rose out of the darkness. Johnny could feel his face glowing red.

"I see," said the Irishman after his laughter subsided.

"I'm sorry for laughing, laddy, but you had us worried there for a while." A few more chuckles came from the darkness.

"Worried 'bout what?" Johnny ask.

"Ah, nothin' lad, nothin at all. Now ye were sayin' 'bout yeer feelin' somethin'. Me thinks ye be enamored, laddy."

"Enamored?"

"Ah, well, love, me boy. Those'er the feelin's of first love. The feelin's, almost spiritual, that flows 'twix boy and girl without even touchin' one another when the chemistry is right. Like an elixir so powerful it almost makes ye float. The strong affection that wells up from the very depths of yeer bein'."

"But she didn't even say anything to me," Johnny said.

"Ah, but 'tis not what *she* says or does, laddy. Tis what yeer body and mind sees and hears that makes the difference. Love is a beautiful thing, laddy, but like an elixir it must be sipped a little at a time and can't be rushed. Move too fast and ye chase it away. Move too slow and it slips away. Love is fleeting, love is forever. 'Tis fickle, 'tis coy, 'tis mysterious. Love needs patience, nay, love is patience!

"There is the love of God and Jesus and Mary, love of mother and father, love of ground cherry pie, but, first love of boy and girl, aye laddy, the tenderest.

"There is the love ne'er partaken of, a look in passing, eyes meet and hold one another, a smile secures it.

"There is passionate love of man and wife the memory of which never fades, and is never forgotten," the Irishman's voice drifted off and silence remained in the hold.

· "Do you miss your wife and family?" Johnny asked, breaking the silence.

"Aye, lad, I do indeed. We all do. Someday when I find my way in this country, I shall bring them here t'be together again."

"Here, here," came from the darkness of the hold.

Chapter Four

THE NEGROES

Three bells sounded the signal to land. The *Mary Louise* came around to starboard and approached the wharf at Cincinnati, the "Queen City of the West" as it was known. Activity on the wharf came alive as drays scurried about, preparing to load and receive freight. Passengers pressed forward in anticipation of boarding.

On board the ship the crew gathers on the forecastle as the broad stage is run out over the bow, a deckhand stands at the end of it with a coil of rope ready to pitch it to one of the dock crew. Steam screams from the gauge-cocks as smoke rolls out of the stacks, a bell rings, the wheels stop, then reverse. The *Mary Louise* eases into the wharf and stops.

The passengers prepared to off-board and the mate began his constant shouting of orders at the roustabouts to move cargo off and on the ship.

Johnny had never seen such a busy place as Cincinnati, populated by 115,000 souls, with it's many buildings along the river and ascending the slope beyond. Horse drawn carriages and freight wagons were in constant procession as hooves and wheels clopped and clanged on cobble stone streets. The riverfront docks teemed with workers and passengers each seeming to have his or her own predetermined task or destiny, each undeterred by the other. Johnny recalled he hadn't observed much at Pittsburgh, considering his abrupt introduction to the *Mary Louise* and his imprisonment below decks. He would see as much of Cincinnati as one could from the deck of the *Mary Louise* under the vigilance of the mate; Johnny's knife still tucked in one side of his belt and a flint lock hand gun in the other.

The mate kept watch of the Irish roustabouts, for their escape attempts were more imminent to him than those of the Negroes. He reasoned that the Negroes were more resigned to their fate and less motivated to escape. They would be more easily spotted and hunted down than the Irish who would blend into the crowd on any of the docks or towns along the rivers. Ohio being a slave free state, however, the Negro slaves were made to stay below decks, out of sight, while the Irish, claimed by the ships company as paid labor, were used to load and unload lumber and merchandise.

Darkness had settled over the decks of the *Mary Louise* when the last of the merchandise bound for the frontier was loaded aboard. The decks of the boat as well as the dock were lighted by oil lamps, casting dim light and heavy shadows. Johnny noticed the opened hatch door to the hold where the Negroes quarters were located. A row of Irish immigrants appeared to be shielding the door from the view of the mate.

Just then a scuffle broke out on the dock just aft the *Mary Louise*. Two dock workers, it appeared, were about to settle a disagreement. With knives drawn at arm's length they began to circle one another, looking for an opening to move in for a thrust. The mate, the first to enjoy a bloody fight to the death, moved aft of the boat for a better look.

Johnny looked back at the Irishmen and noticed Negroes pulling themselves up and out of the hold and moving swiftly and quietly across the deck behind the row of Irishmen to the stack of lumber.

Johnny looked puzzled at one of the Irishmen who glared back with a frown and a quick toss of his head for Johnny to look away. Johnny looked back quickly toward the knife fight. Blood had not yet been drawn and by all appearances it looked like none was going to be, for as fast as the fight had begun it broke up. As if on signal, the two contestants turned from each other and walked away.

The mate grumbled something and turned around to find the Irishmen standing around, appearing to have been watching the same bloodless scene.

"Hey, ya blamed lazy Irish dirt, what're ya about? Git yer backs inta dis load a freight 'fore ah breaks yer haids open."

It was difficult for Johnny to keep his eyes off the stack of lumber. He was bewildered by it and how the Negroes had disappeared into the shadows.

Not sure of what he had just witnessed, he was convinced that whatever was going on would be a matter of serious consequence if the mate were to discover it.

After the freight had been secured and the broadstage drawn, the *Mary Louise* backed out and straightened down toward Cairo and the Mississippi. The mate ordered all hands below decks, except for the night fireman, and locked the hold door. Johnny was quickly at the side of his Irish friend.

"What's goin' on?" Johnny whispered.

"The Underground Railroad's what they call it, laddy." The Irishman expected more questions.

"I don't get it. How does a railroad run underground and what does that have to do with those Negroes I saw disappearin'?"

"I don't understand it either. When last we were here, some German lads came on board as dock hands an' ask us to help them free the Negroes. They didn't ask much of us. We couldn't very well refuse, laddy."

Johnny raised his voice just above a whisper. "Well, why didn't you tell them you wanted free too?"

"We're Irish laddy, that makes us different. They don't think of us as being slaves. We're paid labor as far as they know."

"Oh yeah," Johnny found himself feeling sarcastic, "free upstanding citizens of these here United States. Did you tell 'em you voted for President Fillmore in the last election, huh? You left Ireland to settle for this? Why?"

"We were starving to death by the thousands in Ireland because of the failure of the potato crop. Ya see, laddy, life aboard this boat isn't so bad when you consider where we might be had we stayed in Ireland, though I must confess, laddy, there is a lot I don't understand bout yeer country."

"Pa talked of a famine in Ireland but I didn't know what it meant," Johnny recalled. "But you're in America now. If you're of a mind to stay on this boat and live like this you're sure's hell not of my father's blood. This is the land of adventure and opportunity. Whatever you grew in Ireland you can grow here and a lot more of it. Potatoes, corn or anything you like, but you'll not do it on this stinkin' boat."

Johnny spoke with a muffled voice loud enough for all to hear. "I've got a plan for escape when we reach Westport Landing, but I'll need your help. The Negroes disappeared behind the lumber. How?"

One of the Irishman chuckled a bit, "Not behind the lumber, lad, into it. When we stacked it in Pittsburgh we left a crawl space to a small area in the center."

"Into it!" Johnny exclaimed. "How long do they intend to hide in the lumber?"

Another Irishman explained, "Those blackies are long gone now. While the mate was watching the scuffle on the dock, they slipped over the side into the water in the blackness o' the night."

"A distraction!" Johnny whispered more to himself then the others, "the fight was a distraction."

He thought for a minute, then, "Sure 'nuff the mate will find them missing at Louieville. That's a slave state, I'm told, and those blackies'll be expected to be on deck. The mate is certain to know you must have helped, or at least knew about the escape. Your lives will be in danger."

"Nay," the Irishman responded confidently, "the mate will need us all the more since he will no longer have the Negroes."

"Sounds like you have it all figgered out," Johnny said, "'cept fer one thing. They hang run away slaves in the south and the people who help 'em. The mate will use you until you get to New Orleans. After that, well, you figger it out."

In the darkness of the hold muffled curses could be heard and someone said, "Damn, I knew we shouldn't have stuck our bloody necks out."

"How does life aboard the *Mary Louise* seem now, gents? You have no choice, we escape at Westport Landing. Are you with me?"

One at a time they agreed.

"Freedom, laddy," a voice came from the darkness. "The freedom to come and go as yee please. To shape yeer own future. You think we be able to grow potatoes in this place 'ee call California, laddy?"

"Don't know," Johnny said as he prepared to bed down for the night, "but this is a mighty big country. I'm sure, somewhere   between Westport Landing and California you might find a place to grow a tater er two."

"That's good, laddy, that's good," another voice said, "I feel hope for the first time since I left Ireland."

Still another voice said, "Thank 'ee, laddy, 'ee gave us something to live for again. Something to fight for."

"Now that sounds more like the Irish of my pa's kinfolk."

"What's your plan for escape, laddy?" his friend ask.

"I'm not sure yet. Got to learn more about the pressure system on the boiler, but I think I can cause a ruckus in the boiler room that'll have the crew busy for awhile."

"Careful, laddy. Ya tinker too much with those boilers an' they might blow on ye and we all be dead."

*****

The mate rousted the men in the hold every morning long before dawn by slamming the hatch door a few times and hollering curses and insults. This morning was no exception, but Johnny   was already on his feet anxious to get to the boiler room to stoke the furnaces and await an opportunity to slip behind the lumber to find the hiding space.

Johnny stepped into the fresh air on the deck, leaned his head back and took the crisp morning air deep into his lungs. Clouds filled the night sky, covering the earth like a blanket.

Must be a storm comin', he thought. Looking up at the passenger decks, his mind flirted with images of the pretty girl. The night lanterns, aided by a north wind, cast moving shadows across the worn planks toward the forecastle as he moved toward the boiler deck to relieve the night fireman.

Another night of cold planks of the hold floor and the chilled morning made welcome the warmth in the boiler area. He checked the furnaces that had just been stoked. The pressure was approaching normal.

The engineer came over and checked the pressure. Johnny was pleased with himself at how well he had figured out the relationship between the amount of fuel required to reach a certain temperature. He had become quite proficient at maintaining the constant pressure the engineer insisted upon. The needle indicator had begun to stick since his near catastrophe a few days before and he had to bang his knuckles on the glass cage to free it. Johnny was growing impatient with the pressure gauge. The engineer agreed to look into the problem, but just as quickly forgot it. More often now Johnny would find the engineer asleep in the middle of the day with an uncorked jug, spending more of his time with his jug of spirits and less time looking over Johnny's shoulder.

Several hours into the day the storm approached with gusty winds. The boat, heavily laden with its cargo, rode out the storm well, pitching fore and aft. Having no sea legs, Johnny had difficulty in maintaining his balance in the boiler room. Though his stomach was queasy and unsettled he knew it would be worse down in the stifling hold or wrestling with the elements on deck.

For most of the day the lightning and thunder crashed around the boat. The wind brought a welcome coolness to the furnace room. The deck hands struggled to right tarpaulins against the blowing rain as it raked across the deck and splashed against the hatch covers and top side cargo.

Darkness was upon them when his relief arrived. Johnny advised the night fireman to be watchful of the pressure gauge. Now he would use the cover of darkness and inclement weather to search the stack of lumber for the passage way made by the Irishmen and used by the Negroes to escape.

Before leaving the boiler room Johnny threw a blanket on the engineer, who had been snoozing in the corner, to ward off the night chill. The engineer snorted and grinned as he clung to his jug, dead to the world.

The activity on deck was closer to chaos than confusion. The wind-whipped rain tore up canvas covers and tried to take everything with it not nailed or tied down. The mate was kept busy fighting the blowing rain and shouting orders as Johnny stepped up next to the stack of lumber, then quickly behind it. In the scarce light he could barely make out a tunnel-like gap between the stacks of freshly cut planks. He went immediately to his hands and knees and crawled into the tunnel.

Johnny could see nothing in the dim light. As he approached what he thought must be the center of the stack, he sensed the presence of something; or someone. He froze, thinking the mate had seen him enter the tunnel and followed him in. Or, could the mate have discovered this tunnel already and be in here somewhere waiting to run him in with his knife?

Johnny knelt, motionless, listening, trying to determine movement in a dim shaft of light that shown from somewhere above, near the center of the stack.

For a moment he thought he heard a thumping coming from somewhere up ahead, but realized it was only the sound of his own heart beating in his ears. He inched forward. Now someone was so close he could hear uneven breathing. On the edge of panic, he waited for the cold steel blade to cut into him. At the same instant, two faint white objects seemed to float in midair a few inches from his face. Startled, he reared back like a horse sighting a rattlesnake and banged his head on the planks.

"Owoo. . ." His cry of pain cut off by a hand that wrapped around his throat. Johnny grasped the wrist, trying to find the arm that held the knife. Then he realized both hands were on his throat. He grabbed both wrists and pulled them away, twisting them.

A groan of pain came from the darkness. Johnny knew it wasn't the mate he had just wrestled. The two white objects he now determined to be eyes set in a very dark face.

"What the . . . !" Johnny exclaimed. "Who're you?"

"Picker be mah name, boss," a voice whispered.

"Well, Picker, ya near scert the life outta me."

"Wull, Ah ascert too. Who're you and what you doin' sneakin' in here like dat."

"Names Johnny Farrell from Cornplanter on the Allegheny. You're one of the Negro slaves. I thought all you escaped last night. Why are you still here?"

"Ah was dah last in line to go over dah side. Ah waited too long. Ah ascert of de water. Doin' know how to swim. The mate turn 'round too soon. If Ah made a move he would've seen de others so Ah stayed back. Been hidin' here since. A girl, one of dah passagers, been throwin' me some 'tatoes down dat shaft. You kin see dah passager deck from dere," he explained, pointing toward a shaft between two stacks. "Ah guess she figgered out what was hapnin' lass night. Guess she figgered Ah'd go over dah side tonight. Ah still ascert of dat water."

"Was the girl pretty?" Johnny asked, showing more excitement than he meant.

"Yeah. Wid de curls."

"Yeah," Johnny whispered. "Can ya hold out here a few more days?"

"Yeah, sho'. Why?" Picker answered.

"When we dock in Westport Landing, I'm gonna cause a distraction. There's gonna be men scatterin'. We can make a break fer it then. You won't even hafta get yer feet wet."

"What kinda de-straction, and what about da mate? He mighty good wit dat gun and knife of his and he likes to use 'em. Ah seen'em do it," Picker said with a shudder.

"Yeah, he do present a problem, but if things work out as planned he might be too busy. Too distracted you might say," Johnny chuckled.

"An what if dey don't work out as planned?" Picker worried.

"Well then, you won't be any worse off then you are now," Johnny said, then added, "and I'd say you was in a perdicerment now."

"Yeah, a real 'perdicerment' Ah'd say," Picker agreed.

*****

The following day they arrived at Louisville. The order was given by the pilot to come around to larboard. Bells clanged, steam hissed, and paddle wheels roiled the water as the steamer came to a stop along side another steamboat loaded with prairie schooners. The customary hustle of passengers and dock crew awaited the broad stage for embarking and debarking. The mate flipped open the hold door to the slave quarters and began barking orders for their presence on deck.

Johnny was tending the furnaces, removing ashes into metal buckets to be thrown overboard later. He heard the mate hollering and eased across the boiler room to a gap between the slats of the wall and watched the mate as he peered into the empty hold.

Apparently not wanting to attract attention to the situation, the mate turned immediately and commanded the Irish roustabouts to the task of loading and unloading the freight.

Looking toward the furnace room he hollered, "Farrell, git yer arse out here!"

"Yes sir!" Johnny said as he stepped out of the furnace room.

"Git yer back into da task at hand. Help these scum," he ordered.

While working on deck Johnny saw the prairie schooners lined up on the freight deck of the boat next to them. He noticed they were much smaller than the Conestoga wagons used for hauling freight in Cornplanter. Smaller and lighter, he supposed, for the long haul across the land on the trail west. His spirits lifted with the thought.

When the loading was completed, the mate ordered the roustabouts below decks and Johnny back to the furnace room. Johnny watched as crew members hustled his Irish friend toward the mates quarters on the main deck. He was sure the mate meant to question him about the disappearance of the slaves.

Within a few hours they were underway again through the new canal built around the Falls of the Ohio where the Ohio River dropped twenty-four feet in three miles, causing dangerous rapids that had inhibited steamboat travel in the past.

The current pulled them down the Ohio River past the notorious Cave in Rock on the Illinois side where, it was rumored, pirates lured passengers and crew of flatboats and keelboats into the cave where they robbed and killed them.

A red western sky cast a glow over the passenger deck. Johnny ambled slowly near the wood stack after the night fireman relieved him. Casually looking around, he slipped under the wood overcropping into the tunnel under the pile.

"Psst, Picker," Johnny whispered, "you doin' awright in here?"

"Yeah, but ah gots to git outta here, Johnny. It's startin' to work on mah bones, makin' me feel like an ol' man."

"Hang on, ol' man, only a couple more days and we be free. Just keep thinkin' about freedom."

"Dats all Ah been thinkin' of, but Ah scert. Ah hear screamin' comin' from dah mates quarters 'while ago."

"A woman screamin'?" Johnny asked.

"No. Sound like a man, bein' hurt on purpose."

"Tortured?" Johnny asked startled. Then he remembered the Irishman being led away. "See ya later, Picker. Say a prayer things work out as I plan."

"Ah way 'head of you dere, Johnny," Picker answered.

Johnny crawled out from under the lumber and, seeing nothing unusual, hurried to the roustabout's hold in fear of what he would find.

In the dark hold, lit only by the light of one small candle, he heard the moans of someone in pain. He felt his way along the hull to his berthing location.

"Johnny?" someone whispered in a raspy voice.

"Yeah, that you?"

"Y-Yes, laddy," the Irishman whispered, hanging onto Johnny's arm, "the mate wanted to know what happened to the Negroes. I-I told 'em I didn't know so he began to beat me." The Irishman stopped, took a deep breath then continued. "H-He beat me bad, la-laddy," he gasped, "I had to tell 'em."

Johnny gently put his hand to the Irishman's face and felt what he knew at once was blood on swollen and broken flesh and bone.

He tore the sleeve from his shirt. Dipping it into the water bucket, He gently wiped the face.

"T-Then he ask me 'bout you, lad. He knows yeer plannin' to escape. He wanted to know how you plan to do it. I-I'm sorry, lad, I told him what I knew. I could-couldn't help it lad," the Irishman began to sob.

"What's done is done. Lie down now and rest."

"He's g-going to kill ye, laddy, before we get to Westport Landing," the Irishman said through his tears. "And it's all me own fault."

"No, you rest now. I thank God you're still alive."

"Tell me 'bout Cornplanter on the Allegheny, laddy. Is it a good place to live? Is it like Ireland, did your father say?"

Johnny made a pillow as best he could from the straw on the floor and laid the man's head back. He continued to daub his face while he considered the questions.

"Well, my pa never said too much 'bout Ireland," Johnny started, then thought better of it. "I never been to Ireland, but, ya never seen nothin' till you've seen the hills of Pennsylvania where they slope, in some places like a wall, to the banks of the Allegheny River. In the summer when the trees are so thick on the mountain they look like carpets of green wool from a distance and in the fall they have all the colors of the rainbow. Shades of yellow, orange and red."

Johnny paused for a moment as he thought of the Alleghenies and his ma and pa. For the first time since his enslavement on the *Mary Louise*, he had time to think about everything and what had become of his life, which was now in imminent danger.

The Irishman coughed and rolled a little to his side.

Johnny continued, "Then sometimes on a winter morning you wake up and the snow covers the ground and clings to the barren trees and bends the pine brows . . ." He stopped, sensing something strange within the hold of the boat. A faint glow in the blackness perhaps, and a cold chill.

· A voice came from out of the darkness, "Put your hand under 'is nose, lad."

"What?" Johnny asked.

"Your hand lad, place it under 'is nose and tell me what 'ee feel."

Johnny put his hand under the Irishman's nose.

"I feel nothin', he said, "nothin'. God in heaven, I feel nothin'."

"He's gone back to bonny Ireland, lad."

Muffled voices came from the darkness within the hold, "In the name of the Father, the Son, and the Holy Ghost."

Johnny made the Sign of the Cross as his eyes burned with tears.

"We'll take 'im now, lad," a voice said as he heard roustabouts shuffling forward.

"What're you gonna do with him?" Johnny asked.

"We'll say a prayer for 'im and then 'eft 'im over the side."

"What? No!" Johnny gasped.

"If we let the mate do it he will gut 'im before he 'efts 'im so that he sinks to the bottom, lad. If we do it, body whole, he will float and per'aps a kind soul will find 'im and give 'im a Christian burial."

Johnny gave up his Irish friend, seeing the merits of what he was told.

The roustabouts lifted the slight body and struggled up the ladder out of the hold with it, knowing the mate would not interfere with the disposal of the body.

Johnny's thoughts went back to his religious training under Father Slattery at Vogelbacher Settlement when he came on horseback to Cornplanter to teach and offer Mass. Johnny remembered a sermon he once gave about the frailty of life and the finality of death. The words that meant little at the time, now held deep meaning. "...from the moment of conception, to the first wisp of breath that sustains it, to the last gasp that ends it," he had said, "life is precious; death is eternal . . . "

In a short while Johnny heard the faint splash of the Irishman's body in the water. He shuddered and wept.

Chapter Five

TRIALS ON THE MISSISSIPPI

All the tributaries to the Ohio River for 981 miles of its length from Pittsburgh to Illinois added to the enormity of the river. By the time it spilled into the Mississippi at Cairo, Illinois the river, swollen by spring run off, inundated its banks.

Cairo endures its annual spring flood. With the river front docks moved inland and a channel dug for the purpose of accommodating the keel of the steamboats, the *Mary Louise* eased into a wharf.

While docked, Johnny helped with the loading and unloading of cargo. The great Mississippi River stretched across the horizon under grey skies. There seemed to Johnny no end to the water. Most shops and homes could only be approached by small boats, canoes, or rafts. The inhabitants of Cairo, named for its similarity to Cairo, Egypt at the convergence of two rivers, seemed to take it all in stride. *A normal spring in Cairo*, the word went on the decks of the *Mary Louise* as Johnny helped load and unload trade goods to and from high ground.

Hides and furs from the land beyond the frontier headed for tanneries and clothing factories in the east and barrels of molasses and flour from mills in the Illinois farming communities headed for the frontier.

"And potatoes," Johnny mumbled, reminded of his hunger.

The lack of proper nutrition and overwork had sapped Johnny's strength. He had noticed the gaunt faces and low energy of the Irish immigrants. They moved slow with little ambition. Johnny understood why few had ever attempted escape or even considered it. Aside from the fear of the mate catching them was the knowledge that they didn't have the strength to swim any distance or run very far.

Though Johnny had no knowledge of proper nutrition, he knew what his body kept telling him. He craved vegetables at the moment. Other times he would dream of venison his pa roasted over a camp fire. He thought of Picker and the boiled potatoes the girl had thrown to him.

Johnny looked back at the lumber stack and above at the railing of the passenger deck. The girl leaned on the railing, seeming to watch the work progress on the lower deck. She held nothing in her hands. Johnny imagined Picker enjoying his meal of warm boiled potatoes. While engrossed in the thought of that boiled potato, Johnny heard a loud crack and felt a sharp pain at the back of his skull.

In the next instant, he found himself face down on the decking planks with blood running from his nose. The mate had just clubbed him with the broad side of a barrel stave on the back of the head.

"Ya likes da purty gals, do ya? Ah know what you were thinkin'," the mate growled.

Johnny felt his temper flare and he came up from the deck fists flying wildly.

A mistake indeed.

The mate caught Johnny's right arm mid-swing with the barrel stave and hammered a fist to his mid-section bending him over in pain. The mate brought his knee up into Johnny's face. Falling backwards, Johnny crashed to the deck.

The mate, excitement showing on his face, pulled his left booted foot back ready to drive it into Johnny's twisting body.

A shout came from the decks above.

"That'll be enough, mate." It was the captain. "He'll do us no good with busted ribs. I think you let him know his eyes are to remain off the passenger deck and on the work at hand."

"Aye sir," the mate grumbled.

The mate grabbed Johnny by the hair and pulled him

to his feet. "Ya git yer arse into da furnace room, pig," he barked as he shoved Johnny toward the furnace room door. Johnny stumbled and fell to the deck beside the stack of lumber.

The mate returned to main decks and ordered the roustabouts back to work. "Move dat gangplank f'rward der, lively now, no, no aft, aft ya dimwits, aft. Now f'rward a little. Bring'er in now, sit'er down."

A whisper came from the stack of lumber. "Heeey, Johnny. Here."

A boiled potato rolled across the deck in front of Johnny's face. He quickly scooped it up and tucked it into his shirt. He picked himself up and stumbled through the boiler room door. Once inside he pulled the potato from his shirt and greedily devoured it. Then he gave thought to where it had come.

"Thanks, Picker," he mumbled through bloodied lips.

His feeling of stupidity tempered by an aching body, he felt foolish for having given the mate an excuse to pommel him.

"A fellow don't eat he don't have no strength to fight," he said.

"Whazzat," the engineer slurred from a corner where he sat holding his jug. "Wha' happen to ya, lad. You don' look so good."

"Nothin' ol' man. Go back to sleep."

"Aye you say, back to sleep," the engineer stumbled getting to his feet, "time for little sleep for either of us now. Up to this point you've had it easy stokin' that furnace. We been sailin' with a half head of steam with the current down the broad Ohio; save for the time you like to blowed us outta the water. Now we'll need a full head of steam 'cause we sail against the current all the way to Saint Louie and Westport Landing. This time of the year the Mississippi and Missouri run fast an' deep which means you will be spending much of your time feedin' the furnaces. I hope this ol' boat'll hang to."

"Why wouldn't it?" Johnny asked.

"Cause it's old. Seen many trips up these ol' rivers."

Johnny ladled water from the water bucket and poured it over his head.

It wasn't the thought of hard work that Johnny minded. He could even understand why the rest of the crew enjoyed the adventures of the steamboat life, but the treatment which he and his Irish friends received and the conditions under which they existed aboard this boat kept his mind on his plan for escape.

He wiped the already clotting blood from his face and hair with the tail of his shirt.

"Sir," Johnny ventured reasoning with the engineer, "I can work a lot harder with proper nourishment. Do you 'spose you could get me some extra rations?"

"Aye lad," the engineer had set back down in his corner, his eyelids were beginning to droop, "see what I kin do. Can't promise nuttin. I got no pull on this boat. I owe too many for coverin'."

"Thank you, sir," Johnny said not sure that the engineer would remember the conversation.

The *Mary Louise* lay overnight at Cairo waiting for late deliveries of milled goods. By midmorning the next day, under a full head of steam, straightened up against the eddies and currents created by the confluence of the Ohio and the wide and muddy Mississippi.

Heretofore the *Mary Louise* had been using coal for fuel which was in good supply from the Pennsylvania and Virginia coal fields, but by the time they reached the Mississippi the coal supply was low in the boat's tender. The source of fuel would now be wood purchased from suppliers along the banks of the river.

After a day's steaming up the Mississippi they began to ease toward the bank on the Missouri side. The soundings were heard being called by the leads man to the pilot.

"Mark three! Mark three! Quarter-less-three! Half twain!" the water grew shallow as they drew nearer the wood-yard on the west side until the leads man called eight feet. The pilot rang the bell to signal the engine room. The paddle wheels slowed than stopped. The boat sidled gracefully into a bar and held.

A wood-flat was poled out from the wood-yard and tied aft the *Mary Louise*. The purser paid the wood-yard man and they were again underway.

The engineer explained the difference between the burning of coal and wood to Johnny. "Coal burns hotter and longer," he said, "therefore there is less need of stokin'. Wood burns faster and requires almost constant stokin', so you been relaxin' on this cruise till now. An' me? Well I'll have to stay alert. Aye, the whole crew will be on the watch day and night for sawyers and planters."

"Sawyers and planters?" Johnny asked.

"Yeah, big dead trees that float just under the surface and rise up sometime like a giant monster with it's limbs like tentacles reaching out. They been known to push boats back down stream, or get caught up in the paddle wheels. Planters? Well, that's a tree trunk that wedges it-self into the river bottom at one end and floats with the current at the other. A boat runs into one of them and it comes right through the hull."

The hills along the banks of the river were alive with the fresh foliage of spring. As they steamed north, the chimneys of the old steamer belched smoke from roaring furnaces below. Furnaces that kept temperatures up in the boilers. Boilers that provided steam for the engines that kept the paddle-wheels churning the muddy waters of the awesome river. The pilot and every crewman, ever watchful of drifting dead logs and giant trees that had caved in and washed away from the banks of rivers many miles ahead.

A crewman on the forecastle saw it first.

Looming out of the gray shadows of dusk, coming on fast, a huge freshly uprooted tree adorned with all it's fo-liage floated on the water dead ahead. The pilot rotated his wheel into a turn to starboard, but before the boat could respond the tree crashed directly into the bow. The *Mary Louise* shuddered, stopped dead, and began to drift backward. Passengers and crewmen tripped, fell and stumbled. The tree, with it's giant limbs, centered the force of the river directly on the bow. The crewman on the forecastle fought, trying to free himself from the tangled mass of the tree.

The pilot yelled through the speaking tube at the engineer, "Let 'er have every once you've got! Hurry now!"

Johnny and the engineer picked themselves up from the floor where they had been hurled. The engineer ran to the throttles and threw them all the way forward.

"Keep stokin' those furnaces!" he yelled at an already exhausted Johnny.

Steam hissed from the boilers into the engine cylinders. The engine roared. The paddle-wheels dug into the water and the boat lurched and groaned. The mate bellowed orders at the crewmen while their axes chopped at limbs. The pilot turned his wheel first one way than another in an attempt at dislodging the tree.

"A planter?" Johnny yelled at the engineer.

"No, you'd a heard a tremendous crunch and tearing if it were a planter!" he yelled back over the roar of the engines, "an' you'd be up to your neck in water by now! That is a live uprooted tree dead on the bow! A big'un too I might add, to stop us like that!"

The engineer looked first at the gauges and the boiler seams, then at the drive shafts with a worried expression.

The boat shuddered.

"Let'er drift for while, you fool!" the engineer said of the pilot, "this ol' boat can't take much of this any more! Come apart at the seams, it will!"

Johnny could feel the boat lifting and rocking sideways, then, all of a sudden, it lurched forward.

"We're free!" the engineer yelled.

"Ease'er off down there, engine room. Where the hell ya think your goin' to the races or somethin'?" came the words with laughter from the speaking tube.

"Funny!" the engineer frowned. "You'll find plenty to laugh at someday," he muttered.

"The pilot don't sound too worried bout things," Johnny reminded the engineer.

"I'd not be surprised if he seen that tree comin', or at least didn't do much to avoid it," the engineer noted.

"Why?" Johnny asked.

"Pilots are a conceited bunch. They enjoy the contest for the sake of winning and strut their abilities at piloting before the passengers and crew who believe them heroes of a sort. Truth be told it would take more ability to have maneuvered the boat to miss the tree. But then, there would not have been nearly the drama, now would there?"

"Got to admit," Johnny allowed, "it was a bit excitin'."

"Excitin'!" the engineer retorted, "well you be as ignorant as that pilot. I tell you, this old engine ain't gonna take much more of that foolery, nor these boilers. Aye, the pilot boasts of his skills as handler of boats, demands performance. To the captain, time lost is money lost to the company. The passengers are impatient to reach their destinations. I tell them, 'indulge me, this is an old boat she needs gentleness'. They laugh at me, or ignore me. Humph," he grumbled. He grabbed up his bottle and slid down the wall of his favorite corner and sat.

In the order of import, Johnny knew, the engineer had little sway. There would be no respite for the *Mary Louise*.

Chapter Six

FAREWELL MARY LOUISE

Gray early morning skies hung low over the Mississippi River. A drizzle dampened the decks of the *Mary Louise*. Coming in sight of the port of St. Louis the pilot and crew relaxed their vigil for wayward trees and floating debris to prepare for docking as the mate shouted orders. The excitement on board grew more intense with the passengers scurrying about, collecting their belongings and saying goodbye to new found friends while they lined up to debark.

"Throw in the pitch pine!" the engineer shouted at Johnny. "We're about a mile or so off Saint Louie. Let 'em know we're comin!"

Johnny trembled with excitement. He loaded the furnaces with the pine then ran out on deck to watch the city of St. Louis come into view. The pilot and engineer, communicating through the speaking tube, brought the ship toward port.

Johnny looked through the mist at the hills on either side of the Mississippi as they slipped slowly by, clothed in spring foliage. Suddenly, looming out of the fog, the port at St. Louis came into view. People busied themselves on board the *Mary Louise*, but now Johnny could see the activity on the docks. Crowds lined the roped dock, waving towards him. At first he wondered why or at who they could be waving. He turned toward the passenger decks and saw the passengers waving back. He then looked at the plumes of smoke, he had created with the pitch pine, belching from the stacks. A flush of pride swept over him as the great old boat drew nearer the port in all it's glory, whistles blowing, bells ringing. Johnny now thoroughly understood the romantic side of the river boat life. They were, at the moment, the center of attention in all the world. He could feel the vainglory of the pilot now, as he expertly maneuvered his boat to dock, and the crew as they tethered the boat and ran out the planks.

Upon the faces of the passengers waiting to board, however, he saw something he had heretofore not noticed. They were faces filled with exuberance for they had reached the frontier of a young and exciting country, the beginning of a new life for each of them. There were expressions of excitement, apprehension, and resolution shared by the many emigrants from different parts of the country, preparing to load their wagons on board the *Mary Louise*. Wagons loaded with everything they owned.

Johnny asked questions of the menfolk as they came aboard. Some were headed for California and Oregon others for Santa Fe. Mules, horses, oxen, boxes, barrels, and crates were loaded on board.

For the remainder of the trip to Westport, Johnny would be full time in the furnace room and bunking there. The roustabouts would sleep on deck or anywhere they could find, for the holds were crammed full with everything imaginable. Exhilaration grew within Johnny. His dream of venturing to California within his grasp. He shared the enthusiasm of the emigrants, for he now recognized he was one of them.

It was well after dusk by the time the passengers and their trappings were loaded on board. The *Mary Louise* made her way up the Mississippi a few miles before entering the mouth of the Missouri.

The engineer brought Johnny a bowl of Brunswick stew from the passenger mess. "Here," he said, "you're gonna need the strength. You may have to swim before this voyage is over."

Navigation on the turbulent Missouri river was difficult for the best of pilots and their steamboats, but it would prove an exceptional course for the aging *Mary Louise*. The engineer, keenly aware of her limitations, became obsessed with the engines and the boilers. He checked them every few minutes and kept his bottle hidden behind some boxes near the drive shafts, tossing back a good swallow every now and then.

At full steam against the current of this muddy river, so heavily laden that water splashed over her gunwales, the old steamboat gained only a few knots per hour. The paddle wheels rolled deep in the swift moving waters of the Missouri. The engines worked constantly at maximum power. The engineer sank deeper into his drunken stupor and Johnny kept pouring on the wood, eyeing the gauge.

Soon the night fireman came to relieve him. When Johnny left the furnace room he quickly scanned the deck for the mate, seeing instead a mass of confusion. He wanted to see how Picker was holding up. He slipped into the stack of lumber unnoticed, carrying the Brunswick stew to share with Picker.

"Hey. Picker, you there?" Johnny whispered into the darkness under the lumber.

"Course I here. Where you think I be, dancin' on dah maindeck?" Picker grumbled.

"Aaah, you're gettin' sour as a crabapple," Johnny teased. "Here I got vittles for you. The engineer got me a bit of Brunswick stew, I saved you some."

"Dats kinda you, Johnny. You sho' you wan' give it up? You needs dah strength fo' dah workin'."

"You gave yer potatoes to me when you had nothin' else, Picker. Eat up, it'll improve yer atteetude."

"Ah gots a bad feelin' bout somethin' goin' wrong, Johnny."

"What do you mean? I've got everything figger'd out. When you hear a commotion git ready to scramble out of here," Johnny said. "Just don't go in the direction of the boiler room cause you might git your hiny singed by the steam that'll be rollin' out of there," he added with a chuckle.

"Ah doin mean dat. Ah knows you gots dat figgered out, Johnny, you a smart boy, you is."

"Well thank you, Picker, but what do you mean then 'bout somethin' goin' wrong?"

"Ah doin know, Johnny, but Ah gots a awful strong feelin' bout somethin' bad hapnin'," Picker said as he gazed into the darkness, fingering the stew from the clay bowl.

"Ah, yer jest spooky. Been in this dark hole too long. Everything's gonna be just fine soon's we git off this boat," Johnny assured him.

"Mebbe, Johnny, but dah las' time Ah hadda feelin' like dis is when dey took me from mah mammy and sol' me down dah river. Ah din think nothin' worse could happen to me, till now."

"Twix'd you and the engineer I'm gettin' a case of the spooks, both you talkin' like the Lords a Fate gonna git you."

"Johnny, dat sounds bad. What de 'Lawds a Fate'?" Picker asked.

"Oh, those're spirits, the keepers of death's door, that're always tryin' to take us to our death. I always out smart them though, as you can see," Johnny bragged.

"Ooooh, dat's good. Do dey scare you, Johnny?"

"Sure nuff they do, but you gotta fight 'em. Don't give up. When you git the most scared, you gotta git mad and fight 'em, else you jest lay down and die."

"Ooooh, dat's scary," Picker said, "Ah ain't never seen dese Lawds of Fate."

"That's cause you ain't been scert nuff or close nuff to death's door like I been."

"What dey look like?" Picker asked.

"You'll know'em when you see'em," Johnny assured him. "When you get so scert you turn white as a ghost, you'll see'em."

Picker gagged an impulse to laugh aloud. "Dat take some doin' fo' me."

Johnny realized what he had said. "Yeah, that'd take some kindda scarin', huh?"

They both muffled their laughter when they heard voices just beyond the lumber as passengers walked by.

"You know somethin', Picker?" Johnny said solemnly, "I just been tryin' to cheer you up but I gotta tell you the truth. The truth is I'm kinda worried too. I don't know much 'bout steamboats, but the engineer just plain don't think the *Mary Louise* is gonna make it much further. You ain't seen it, but there ain't much clearance twix your hiny and the water anymore. We took on a whole passel of weight in cargo. I ain't never seen this boat settin' so low in the water. The engineer says the Missouri is a swifter runnin' river then the Mississippi 'specially in the spring and this ol' boat is runnin' at full steam."

"What you sayin', Johnny?" Picker said, handing Johnny back the empty bowl.

Johnny looked around them at the stack of lumber, "Most boards float, Picker. If this boat starts sinkin', climb up on the lumber and ride it out. Don't worry 'bout being seen, everybody will be tryin' to save themselves. They won't give a hoot 'bout no runaway slave."

Picker looked worried at the stack of lumber. "You sho' dey float, Johnny?"

"Sure they do, seen it plenty of times," Johnny said. Then he thought for a moment of the weight the boat had taken on and the engineer worrying over the boilers. He drew a final conclusion.

"Thing is Picker, I don't think we should wait till we git to Westport. I think we should git off this boat tonight. I'm not gonna rig the gage cock as I planned. Just before sunup I'll skitter out here and we can slip into the water and swim for shore.

"My intentions were to help the Irish roustabouts escape, but they lost interest when my Irish friend got beat up and killed."

"Whatta bout de mate?" Picker asked. "He sho' to see us."

"Naw, I'm thinkin' there is so much cargo and emigrants camped on deck now the mate can hardly git out his door," Johnny assured him. "He'll not notice us."

"Are you sho', Johnny?" Picker looked to Johnny for reassurance.

"Sure I'm sure. I gotta git back to the furnace room now," Johnny whispered. "You hang tight, don't git discouraged. We're goin' to be off this boat quicker than a snakes bite. We ain't far from Independence, just a day'er so. We can walk the rest of the way when we're on land, safe and dry. See you in the mornin'."

"But Ah cain't swim, Johnny," Picker reminded him.

Johnny thought for awhile. "You ever watch a dog swim, Picker?" he asked.

"Sho' nuff, Johnny. When I bathed inna river mah dog would swim round me."

"Well, just do the same thing using hand strokes in front of you."

"You sho', Johnny?"

"We ain't got no choice, Picker. Lest you wish to be on this boat when it sinks or blows up. Sounds to me yer gonna have to swim one way or tuther. Best it be at the time of yer own choosin' when I might be of some help."

"You is right, Johnny. Don't worry 'bout me. See you in dah mornin'."

When Johnny returned to the furnace room the night fireman was checking the gauge. He then moved to his corner to read his book. The engineer lay in his corner sleeping restlessly. Johnny laid down in another area and tried to get some rest in spite of the noise of the engines and vibration of the flooring.

*****

Before dawn the night fireman jostled Johnny awake for duty. The engineer dashed about, checking the boilers and engines, mumbling to himself like a man gone daft. The engineer's continued concern stiffened Johnny's resolve. He waited the opportunity then slipped out of the furnace room into the half light of dawn to join Picker.

The emigrants on the decks were beginning to stir amid yawns and grumbles. The oxen and mules were restive. Was it because of an environment completely foreign to them, or did they sense impending danger? Johnny thought as he ducked under the lumber.

"Are you ready, Picker?" Johnny whispered.

"Ah's ready, Johnny, and happy to be gittin' outta dis wood pile."

That familiar dual feeling of fear and excitement began to well in Johnny again. Strange, he thought. The same feeling I had when I first left Cornplanter. Joseph's face swept across his mind and his last words about the Lords of Fate.

"Follow me, Picker. We want to swim to the south bank of the river. That's the side Independence is on. Wouldn't do us no good to end up on the wrong side of this river. Now would it?"

"Sho' wouldn't. Ah doin want to swim dis river twice," Picker assured him.

They emerged from the lumber stack without drawing attention among the emigrants and walked unhurriedly toward the stern of the boat. There was hardly an arm's length of room between the wagons, animals and barrels. The mate was nowhere to be seen, but Johnny had the uneasy feeling he was around somewhere. They slipped past the door to his cabin. Johnny and Picker stepped over and around passengers and crew who were sleeping on the deck flooring. Johnny was stepping over a huge man at the far end of the deck when his foot accidentally kicked the sleeping man in the rump. He moaned and rolled over. Johnny froze in place. Sweat forming on his brow, cooled quickly in the morning air. The man did not awaken. Johnny and Picker cautiously continued on toward the stern.

Picker drew in a hard breath when they reached the stern and he saw the water washing over the gunwales.

"Johnny, dis boat is sinkin'," he whispered.

"Not yet, Picker, it's tryin' its best to stay afloat."

Picker looked off the end of the boat and across the water. In the half light it looked like there was no end to the water. Like they weren't on a river at all but in the middle of an endless ocean. He began to panic. "Johnny," he said, grabbing Johnny's shirt tail. "Ders no end to dat water. Ders no river bank! We be out in dat water fo' dah res' of our lives. Ah can't swim dat far, Johnny! Not even a dog can swim dat far."

"There's a bank there, Picker. I know there is and it ain't far away. You just can't see it in the dark."

"No, no dere ain't." Picker's voice was rising. Johnny knew he had to quell Picker's rising fear before they began to draw attention.

"Picker, we come this far, we can't go back," he whispered. "If we git caught, we'll both be hung. You for bein' a runaway slave and me fer helpin' you."

Picker considered Johnny's logic. Then out of the darkness behind them they heard the unmistakable voice of the mate.

"Who goes thar?" he ask as he came out of the dim shadows. "Well what've we har, out for a night's stroll 're we now?"

He looked startled at Picker, not expecting to find one of his slaves. "Yer one of my niggers." Looking at Johnny then back to Picker, he slowly started to reach for the pistol in his belt.

Johnny turned to Picker with the intentions of urging him over the side, but Picker had already disappeared into the water. Johnny started after him, but stopped and turned around.

Johnny faced the mate who had not yet fully withdrawn the pistol, having been distracted with the sudden disappearance of Picker.

Johnny swung his fist hard with the passion of vengeance, smashing the mate squarely on the jaw, sending him crashing to the deck. Johnny winced from pain in his wrist. He approached the mate who sat on the deck dazed, holding his jaw. He quickly removed his knife from the mate's belt, whirled and dove into the water. Swimming away, he caught up to Picker and found him paddling around in circles.

"C'mon Picker, this way!" he yelled.

"Ah din here no pistol shot, Johnny! What happin'?" Picker shouted as he gasped, coughed and spit water.

"I gave the mate somethin' to remember me bye, Picker! Save yer breath! Yer doin' fine! Follow me!"

Picker fell behind quickly. A pistol shot rang out. The lead ball skipped across the water beside him with sludging smacks.

Johnny turned his head just as Picker swam by. Surprised, Johnny had to take extra strides to catch up with him.

They were closer to the south bank of the river then they realized. Johnny reached the shallows first and sat on the muddy bottom, catching his breath. Picker came swimming up to him, gasping for breath.

"I can't swim much fartha, Johnny," he gasped.

"Best you stand up then b'fore you drown."

"What? You mean?"

"Yup, I'm sittin' on the bottom."

Picker put his hands down and felt the muddy bottom. "Well, Ah say."

They burst out laughing, realizing they were safe. But most important they were free! Tears of laughter became tears of joy, both thinking about what they had accomplished in their own ways to get to where they were. The fears they had to overcome.

"Ha!" a humorous thought occurred to Johnny. "We just swam for freedom, now we have to walk for Independence."

Sitting there on the muddy bottom of the Missouri River with their arms around each other they realized there was now a special bond between them as they watched the *Mary Louise* slowly moving up the river, churning low in the water. The rising sun of a new day glimmered on her roiling wake.

Chapter Seven

LEAVING INDEPENDENCE

Upon their arrival in Independence, after a long walk up the Missouri River, Johnny penned a letter.

Joseph Schill
Volgelbacher Settlement
Clarion County, Pennsylvania

Dear Joseph,

I have seen a side of human   nature,
in my experience on the Mary Louise, of
which no one could possibly be proud. I
have come face to face with prejudice
toward the Irish I never knew existed.

But through my cunning I reign superior
over those who would enslave me. You
cannot enslave, for long, a truly free man.

I am free, and with me I have brought a
Negro to freedom. Him to live his life as
he chooses and me to continue my journey.

God and nature have been good to me.
I am alive and well in Independence,
Missouri, looking to board a wagon train
headed west.

Your friend,
Johnny Farrell
June 1852

After posting the letter, Johnny left Picker by the river while he went to barter with a wagon master for passage on his train.

Fifteen wagons waited in line for word from the wagon master to proceed. Johnny ran in the direction of the lead wagon. Captain Will Manley, the wagonmaster, held up his arm looking over his shoulder down the line of oxen drawn covered wagons. "Wagons ho!" he hollered and moved his hand forward.

"Captain sir!" Johnny shouted at the man well mounted on a strong and impressive dapple gray, "Sir, could I tag along with you? I got no money but I can work my way with you, doin' whatever needs doin'."

"No son," the Captain replied, looking suspiciously at Johnny, "You got no grub, no wagon, no horse. How in tarnation would you survive? We're late getting started as it is, and we got no time to wait for you to garner supplies. Best you wait till next spring. This is the last train out, thanks to our educated Mister Fulbright the second bein' late arrivin'."

A frown of disgust appeared on the captain's face as he mumbled, "Didn't know the diff'rence between Saint Joe and Independence. His money is the only thing that kept him from bein' stranded right here."

"I will survive, sir. No need for you to worry 'bout that. Done a passel of that already."

His attention coming back to Johnny, the wagonmaster acknowledged, "Yes, I expect you have at that by the look of you."

"I'm a fair shot, sir. I could do huntin' for you. Nothin' like fresh venison, you know. I was the best shot ever was back in Cornplanter on the Allegheny." Johnny stretched the truth a little.

Will Manley looked down from his mount, raising his brow, he said, "Well, we could always use a fair shot on a wagon train. Can't say as I'd turn up my nose at a chaw of venison or buffalo hump either."

"And I can walk along as fast as these wagons'll move," Johnny added.

"Well, I'll not be responsible for you, son. You go down the line and ask if anybody has chores for you and wants to accept responsibility. Everybody carries their own weight and pays their own fare on this train."

"There is one other thing, sir," Johnny said, "I got a friend out yonder there who wants to come along. He is a hard worker too sir, just as capable as me."

"Who is this friend and why hasn't he shown himself?" Manley replied, looking over his shoulder.

"Well sir, he is a Negro boy. A runaway slave from . . ."

"Whoa now," Manley cut him off.

"I'll not have any runaway slaves on my train. It appears to me yer a runaway from the law yerself if you're protecting that boy. Did you have a hand in helpin' him escape?"

"Well, yeh, I guess I did," Johnny said.

"Outta here, boy," Manley pointed in the general direction of east, "I want no fugitives from the law on this train."

"We didn't break no laws," Johnny retorted.

"Boy, on my wagon train, I am the law and if I say you've broken it you will be dealt with accordingly. Now off with you, boy. Git before I change my mind and hang you from the next tree I see tall enough."

The wagonmaster turned his mount toward the head of the train. Johnny watched the wagons slowly roll by.

"Good day to you, I'll see you out west someday," he said to the occupants of the wagons, tipping his hat to the ladies among them.

On the second wagon an overweight bespectacled boy, looking in Johnny's opinion to be about twelve, sat beside an overweight lady too well dressed for the trail. The boy leaned forward, squinting at Johnny. Pushing his spectacles up on his nose, he hollered, "Hello! What's your name, sir?"

Johnny was taken back, having never before been called sir. "Names Johnny," he chuckled, "Johnny Farrell from Cornplanter on the Allegheny. And what be your name?"

"Charles William Fulbright the third," the boy replied, "Son of Charles William Fulbright the second, Doctor of Medicine and Education."

The lady setting next to him smiled approvingly at the boy. Johnny instinctively recognized the lady as the boy's mother and was immediately reminded of his own mother. Johnny removed his hat and wished her a good journey. As the wagon rolled by, he said to the boy, "Nice to meet you, Charles William Fulbright the third. Good day to you."

On another wagon a young girl sat on the driving bench between an older man and woman Johnny presumed to be her parents. The girl looked at Johnny and smiled. Instantly Johnny recognized her as the girl on the *Mary Louise* who threw the boiled potatoes down to Picker.

"Hey . . . ," he was moved to say something but thought better of it as the wagon passed.

Most of the folks waved and smiled. They seemed grateful to have someone there to wish them farewell. He noticed the children most of all. Some seemed excited to be underway, some looked forlorn and some were expressionless, but they all were friendly. Except for one boy walking beside a mule drawn wagon, the last wagon in the train.

"Hello," Johnny said. He guessed the boy to be ten or twelve years. "What's yer name?"

"Mathias. Who's askin'?" was the curt answer as the wagon trudged along. The boy didn't wait for an answer. Johnny shrugged his shoulders.

With a strong desire to be going with them, he watched as the wagons clattered slowly into the distance. Feeling forlorn, he walked back to give Picker the bad news.

Picker sat under a tree, gazing across the river. "Ah kin tell by dah look of you we ain't goin' to California dis day," he said as Johnny sat down beside him.

Johnny had already convinced himself to tell Picker the truth. He reasoned Picker might as well get used to the fact that life as a free man was going to have its down side.

"Truth be told, Picker, we're gonna have to do some story tellin' in the future. Me bein' Irish and you bein' a runaway slave has its drawbacks, I'm findin' out. The captain of that train was ready to take me till I told him 'bout you bein' a runaway."

"Wull, Ah kin't change bein' black and you kin't change bein' Irish, Johnny, but we kin change bein' honest."

"How's that?" Johnny asked.

"When Ah was but five year old mah masta gave me to his boy as his pers'nal servant fer life. Ah was his playmate fer eight year. He was five year ol' and his name was Francis. Ah growed to love dat boy as mah veriest own brother. It so happened one day dat Francis, he fell into dah river and Ah couldn't reach him and pull him free. Dah currents was too strong and he drownded."

Picker stopped to swallow hard before he went on. "Ah felt so heart broke and sad. Ah cry fer long time after dat in mah mammy's arms."

"Mah masta, he blamed me cause Francis drownded and he sold me down dah river. Dat's how I come to be on dah *Mary Louise*. Ah never seed mah mammy agin."

Picker buried his head in his arms and his body convulse to his sobs.

"Geez, Picker, I-I'm sorry, that's a sad story I swear." Johnny hesitated, then, "But what does that have to do with us bein' honest?"

"Ah be yer pers'nal man, Johnny," Picker said, wiping tears from his face.

"Oh, I don't know, Picker. I wouldn't know what to do with a pers'nal man."

"Ah don't mean fer real, just to fool people. Like dat wagon masta. He been fine if he knowed you was mah masta. Doin you see?"

"Oh, yes, I b'lieve you're right," Johnny said. Seeing an opportunity, he lay back on the river bank with a piece of grass in his mouth, pulling his hat down over his eyes, he said, "But you know, I ain't never been a slave owner. I need some practice. Let's see now, let's start with my boots, I think they needs a shinin'. Then when you get through with them you can fetch me some vittles." Positioning the hat on his face to block the sun, he continued, "Yep, a fella could git used to this real easy, yes sah, real eas . . ."

"Yipe!" Johnny yelled and sat up directly as Picker stood over him, pouring a hat full of river water on him with one hand and holding a handful of mud in the other.

"Dat's yo' dinner drink, sah, and here's yo' vittles comin' right up."

Johnny rolled over and sprang to his feet, running and laughing towards town with Picker right on his heels.

"What's you runnin' fo', Masta? Ah gots yo' dinner fo' you!"

"I decided I ain't hungry, you eat it!" Johnny pleaded.

Suddenly Johnny stopped. He looked toward a livery stable as Picker stumbled in behind him.

"Look," Johnny said, pointing at the stable.

Picker looked but all he saw was an old man who appeared to be shoeing a horse.

"Ah don't see nothin'," Picker said.

"I see some writin' says 'help needed' that's what I see. I'd be willin' to bet that ol' man needs help."

"Ya think so?" Picker said as he brushed mud from his hands, "Member now, Ah's yo' personal man."

"Oh, I'll not be fergettin' that soon," Johnny teased. "Come on, let's find out."

The old man had just finished shoeing the horse when Johnny and Picker approached.

"Afternoon, sir," Johnny began, "Name's Johnny Farrell from Cornplanter on the Allegheny. Me and my personal man here was lookin' for work and seein' your writin' there says as much, was hopin' you might have some laborin' to be done for an appreciable consideration. Though our true intentions are to provision ourselves for travel to California next spring, we will give you an honest days work till then, if you will, sir."

The old man looked curiously at Johnny, then at Picker. "What do ya mean, personal man?" he asked.

"Oh, yeh, well, my pa gave him to me as a boy. I own him, sir."

"Last I heard, the Allegheny is in Pennsylvany."

"Why, yes sir. That's absolutely right I'm proud to say," Johnny replied.

"Last I heard Pennsylvany was a free state," said the old man.

"Ahh, yes sir, yes it tis at that."

"Then how is it you come to own a slave inna free state?"

Johnny felt trapped in his own lie. He was caught and he knew it. He looked appraisingly at Picker who raised his eyebrows.

"You wantta try the truth now, boy," the old man said. "This a runaway slave you have here, is it not?"

"Yes sir," Johnny said, half ready to make a run for it. He looked at Picker and saw he was already edging away.

"Hold on there now," the old man said. "So happens I am against slavery. I don't believe one man has a right to own another. I do need help here as the sign says. I got kicked by a mule last winter and my hip ails me quite some."

"Very good, sir!" Johnny said. Then, a little chagrined, "I mean about your need of help. Sorry 'bout your hip."

"You can start by cleanin' out those stalls in there and brushing down this horse," the old man said, pointing out the horse he had just shod. "I'll pay yer wages after you work for a month, how much ya git depends on how hard ya work. Till then I'll feed you two meals a day, which will come outta yer first month's wages." Looking suspiciously at Johnny, he said, "You say your name is Farrell? Sounds Irish to me."

"It does, sir?" Johnny said as if questioning his judgement.

Picker broke in, "Mah name is Picker, masta. Where you keep yo' cleanin' tools?"

"You'll find everything required inside in the corner to yer right," the old man said, impressed by Pickers desire to get to work, "an' I ain't your master. You're a free man now. You work for wages. Though I will accept the address of sir or Mister Wheeler from both of you."

"Come, Johnny, wees got us work," Picker said, pulling Johnny by the arm into the barn. "Dis mah first job as a free man."

Johnny and Picker enjoyed working for Mr. Wheeler. Business picked up as word got around that the horses were well groomed and fed at the livery stable and in a timely manner. The old man never again questioned Johnny's being Irish. Johnny was sure he hadn't forgotten about it, but he was satisfied with the work he and Picker performed.

* * * * *

On a sunny afternoon, after a month of working in the livery, Johnny and Picker sat on a fence rail waiting for Wheeler to return from his banking to receive their first wages.

Picker examined an arrowhead he had found in the corral.

"What do you have there, Picker?" Johnny asked.

"Doin know," Picker said, handing Johnny the arrowhead.

"Looks like an ol' flint arrowhead," Johnny surmised. "Keep it for luck, or startin' fires," he said, handing it back to Picker

"Yeah," Picker agreed. "We have luck findin' Mista Wheeler an' workin' for monies. Ah's 'bout to git mah first pay fo' mah work. Ah ain't never been paid b'fo'."

"What're you gonna do with all your money, Picker?"

"Ah gonna save it an' someday Ah'm gonna find mah mammy an' pappy an' buy dere freedom an' bring dem to dah north."

"Ain't you gonna come out west with me next spring?" Johnny asked.

"Ah been thinkin' on tellin' you sooner or later, Johnny. Ah kinda like de ol' man an' Ah kinda likes workin' fo' him. Ah never did have no big yearnin' to go out west. Ah just wanted mah freedom."

"I understand, Picker," Johnny said, "Twern't no dream of yours to start with, goin' west. I'm goin' to miss you though. I guess I got kinda attached."

"Yeah, Ah owes you fo' helping me git free. Don't know how Ah ever repay you fo' dat."

"Shucks, Picker, we helped each other git free. Ahaaa, here comes Mister Wheeler," Johnny said, sliding off the fence.

"Good afternoon, boys."

"Good afternoon, Mister Wheeler," they said.

"You boys have done mighty fine work for me this past month and I promised to pay you accordin' to how hard you worked. I aim to keep my promise. These envelopes contain top wages for a month."

While Johnny and Picker accepted the envelopes and offered their gratitude, a grim expression bridged Mr. Wheeler's brow. Johnny noticed it first.

"Somethin' wrong, Mister Wheeler?" Johnny asked, getting Picker's attention from the money he had just received.

"You boys ever hear of the steamship *Mary Louise*?"

"Sure have, sir," Johnny admitted without hesitation, "That's the boat we escaped from."

"We?" Mr. Wheeler asked. "You mean you both escaped from the *Mary Louise*? Why did you have to escape?" he asked Johnny.

"Well sir, I was hired on in Pittsburgh by the captin but I never got no wages. Word among the roustabouts was that the mate and crew stole the wages and made slaves of the roustabouts."

"That sounds like a lot of hearsay ta me. You got any proof?

"Proof!" Johnny said. "No sir, that's the truth as I know it. Why do you ask, sir?"

"There's a fellow in town asking questions and looking for two boys, one nigger runaway and a white boy who helped him. Fits the description of you two, I'd say."

"Who is this fellow?" Johnny asked.

"Says he's the mate from the *Mary Louise*. Seems the boat blew up at dock side in Westport about the same time you two showed up here, give a day or two."

"Blew up!" Johnny straightened up and looked at Picker whose eyes widened in shock. "Anybody get killed?"

"Oh, yes," Mr. Wheeler answered, "but not as many as could have been. They had just off loaded all passengers and cargo the night before and were getting up steam the next morning. The boiler blew."

"Yup," Johnny said, remembering the engineer worrying, "and I could just 'bout tell you which boiler."

"Oh?" Mr. Wheeler raised his brow in question. "That's pretty much what the mate said. He claims you rigged the gauge cock somehow that caused the boiler to blow. He said one of the roustabouts told him so."

"That's not true, Mister Wheeler," Johnny insisted. "It had been my plan to rig the gauge cock to blow steam into the furnace room as a distraction to help me escape when we docked at Independence. I never did cause we escaped before we got to Independence, cause the engineer had me believin' the boiler would blow before we got there."

Johnny went on to explain everything that happened aboard the *Mary Louise*. About how the mate treated the Irish roustabouts. How the mate got his Irish friend to tell him about Johnny's plan for escape and how his friend died in his arms after being tortured. Picker backed up his story as much as he could.

"Do you believe me, Mister Wheeler?" Johnny asked.

"Yes, I believe you, Johnny, but I have heard nothing that would hold up in a court of law. It's all hearsay, your word against the captain and surviving crew. They claim they paid you a good wage for your labors."

"Court of law!" Johnny exclaimed. "What do you mean a court of law?"

"I guess you don't understand, Johnny. You are wanted for murder."

Johnny stiffened then sank against the fence.

"What dat mean, Johnny?" Picker asked fearfully.

"It means, Picker," Mr. Wheeler explained, "That there is a warrant for Johnny's arrest. When they catch him, they will try him in a court of law. If they find him guilty, which they no doubt will, they will hang him."

Picker gasped, "No, Johnny didn't do no wrong. Johnny's a good boy. I be blowed up and dead now but for Johnny. No, no, no," Picker kept shaking his head.

Johnny wiped perspiration from his brow and stood shaking after hearing Mr. Wheeler's words.

"The engineer will speak up for me," Johnny insisted, "he knew the boiler would blow. He tried to tell them more than once. And the roustabouts they. . ."

"The engineer is dead, son," Mr. Wheeler sadly assured him, "and the roustabouts too. They were trapped below decks."

"Yes, of course, they would have been," Johnny muttered, "and the engineer drunk in the boiler room."

Johnny began to face reality and the gravity of the situation. "In other words, sir, if I give myself up, I'm as good as hung. There's nobody to speak for me but Picker here and they'd hang him the very day they caught him. Being Irish, they'd grant me a 'fair' trial then hang me."

· "I'm gonna ask a lot of you, Mister Wheeler," Johnny continued, "would you take these wages in payment for one of your horses? I won't be needin' a saddle, just a trail rope."

"What are you going to do, son?"

"I'm going to head to California as fast as that horse will take me. I was headed west anyway. My plans ain't changed, just the timin'. Cept now I'm runnin' from the law. Life sure deals a strange hand sometimes."

"It's too late in the season to head to California now son. Bad weather and elements of all kinds will dog your trail all the way, startin' right out there on the plains. Rain storms, sand storms, hail storms, snakes, cholera. Indians won't attack a wagon train, but they have been known to attack lone riders or wagons that got separated. If by some miracle you reach the Sierra Mountains, you'll likely die of the bitter cold weather. The Donner train gives testimony to that."

"Sounds to me like my odds of survival are better there than here, sir." Johnny surmised.

"I'll sell you a horse and provision you best I can if yer mind's made up."

"Suh," Picker stepped up, handing his pay envelope to Mr. Wheeler. "Ah gots no mo' chance here den Johnny," he said. "Ah doin know monies, suh. Would dere be nuff here fo' a horse so's Ah can go wit Johnny?"

"Certainly, more than enough."

"Sure is mighty kinda you, Mister Wheeler. The law will surely be here lookin' for us soon. As I remember there is a law against aiding those wanted by the law. Tell 'em we stole the horses. May as well be hung fer stealin' as murderin'. Hung's hung," Johnny concluded.

"Go on, boys," Mr. Wheeler urged, "pick out a couple of horses from the corral. I'll get some vittles for ya. Best you wait till after dark before you head out. The less folks know the better."

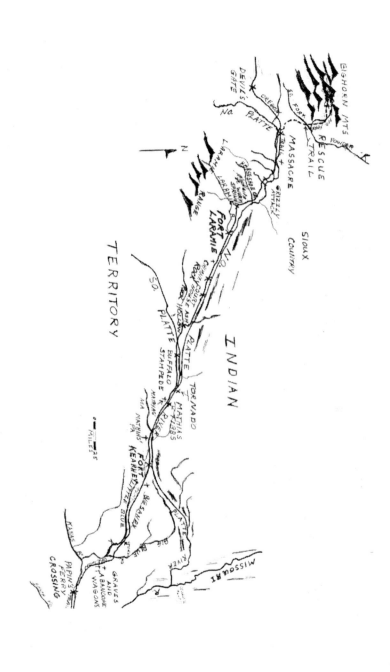

Chapter Eight

BETRAYED

It was past sunset and the quarter moon had not yet risen. Johnny and Picker fashioned ropes into halters for the horses while they waited for Mr. Wheeler to return to the barn with the provisions.

Johnny looked anxiously toward the double doors of the barn. "You know how to ride bare back, Picker?" Johnny asked.

"Doin know how to ride any other way, Johnny."

"Good," Johnny answered out of the dim lantern light as he fidgeted with the lead rope.

An owl hooted out in the yard, putting Johnny on edge and embellishing his impatience. "I wonder what's keepin' the old man?"

"Doin know, maybe he forgots. Ol' folks sometime do you know." Picker picked up on Johnny's nervous fidgeting.

"Yeah, somethin's wrong. I better go see. Hold my horse, Picker."

Johnny edged out of the barn door and looked warily toward the house. A light burned in the main room and he saw movement there. "Hmmm, must've forgot," he murmured and walked hurriedly up to the old house. He was about to call out to the old man when he noticed a horse and carriage on the far side of the house. He walked cautiously up the wooden steps to the front door. The door was open and he heard voices.

"Where are they, Wheeler?"

"First let's have the reward money, Constable. Five hundred the poster said."

"You'll get your money as soon as I have the two of them in my jail."

Johnny froze. Looking into the room he saw a third

man, his face was wrapped in bandages. Must be someone from the *Mary Louise*, Johnny thought.

Then he heard him speak. "Yar stallin', ya scurvy old
man . . ."

Johnny needed to hear no more. He leaped from the
porch and ran to the barn. "Picker!" his harsh half-whis-
per, half-shout hurt his throat. "Hurry! Mount up and
ride. The ol' man sold us out."

Picker connected "sold out" with being "sold down
the river" and immediately knew what to do. He handed
Johnny his lead rope and flung himself upon the horse
and rode out the door of the barn with Johnny riding
hard after him.

Johnny met the constable at the corner of the barn
and figured he must have drawn his attention when he
leaped from the front porch. The constable caught
Johnny's rope reins and for a moment held on, but the
bay mare lurched forward. The constable lost his grip,
falling to the side.

For a moment Johnny thought he was clear, but on
second glance he saw the mate off to his left his revolver
leveled at him. Johnny swung over the side of the little
mare as a shot rang out and a slug whined above him. He
came back astride the horse and followed Picker, who by
now was a distance in front of him.

Picker drew his big gelding to a stop upon hearing
the shot and looked back to see Johnny coming on, waving at him to keep going.

They rode straight through the center of town,
people and horses scattering before them, to the staging
area where the last wagon train departed a month before.

By starlight they could see the trail worn by wagon
wheels. They followed the trail and a short time later
struck the Blue River and, continuing on the well-
marked trail on the other side, rode southwest.

Riding hard, they soon came to a fork in the trail and
reined their horses to a sliding stop. Picker searched the
trail behind them.

"Gots to hurry, Johnny, afo' they catches up. Which way we go here?"

"They won't be catchin' up for awhile, Picker. They had a horse and carriage."

"Who dat, Johnny?"

"The constable and the mate. I saw them parleying with the ol' man 'bout the reward money on our heads," Johnny explained as he held tight rein on his restive horse.

"How much we worth, Johnny?"

"Five hunnered dollars."

"Five hunnered! Sounds like a lot of monies. Is dat a lot of monies, Johnny?"

"Not in my opinion. Not fer my life," Johnny said, studying the two trails.

"Must be the Sante Fe trail goin' south and the Oregon trail west. I have no desire to go south agin. How 'bout you, Picker?"

"South is where my mammy is, Johnny, but, sad to say, so's the hangin' tree. Guess Ah'll only be truly free in the west."

"Let's ride then, Picker. The farther away we git from Independence the better, I'm thinkin'!" Johnny shouted back as he reined his mare around and heeled her forward to a canter.

Johnny and Picker rode hard for days, leaving a wide gap between them and those who would follow. The going was easy and uneventful across the green prairie as the miles passed beneath their horses hooves. At the end of each day they tethered the horses and made cold camp, knowing a fire might attract those in pursuit.

When they arrived at the trail crossing of the Kansas River at Papin's Ferry, they searched out a safe place to cross further up the river. They neither had the ten cents required of each to use the ferry nor did they want to draw attention. A Negro and White traveling together are easily identified if questions should be asked later.

"This looks like as good a place as any, Picker," Johnny said, looking across the turbulent water. "It sure don't look as fierce as the Missouri, not nearly so wide or deep. You can see the bottom."

Picker looked across the river. "Sho' wished we coulda taken dat ferry. Hope dis horse can swim better den me."

"You did a good swim in the Missouri, Picker. You can swim when you put your mind to it. Just stay on your horse's back, he'll get you across. If you can't stay on, slide off and grab his tail. That horse'll have his mind on one thing, gettin' to the other side. That is, if we can get them in the water in the first off."

They edged the fidgety mounts to the river's edge. Johnny didn't give his mare time to consider it before he heeled her into the water. Picker's gelding followed the mare. The water was only up to the horse's elbows, so they had no problem walking the rocky bottom.

Suddenly the river bottom dropped away. Only the horses heads were above water as they lunged against the turbulence. Johnny's little mare drifted downstream while fighting the current. Johnny slipped off the mares back and reached for her tail but missed it. He was swiftly drawn into the rushing flow. Picker had already slipped off the gelding's back and was hanging onto his tail. Johnny watched the gelding as it reached shallow water, climbing out of the river with Picker stumbling after it.

Johnny fought the rushing water, keeping his head above it. Thoughts of his near disaster on the Allegheny gave him confidence that he could handle this river. The Lords of Fate kept their distance. Working his way toward the far bank, he was soon caught up in the bulrushes. Frogs darted and splashed out of his way. Suddenly, a cottonmouth, which had its aim on a frog, found Johnny's hand instead.

"Ahhhh!" Johnny screamed. He splashed through the reeds and tall grass then fell on the bank.

By now Picker had led both horses downstream to where Johnny had come ashore. "Picker, I been bit! I been bit by a water snake."

Picker knelt down and examined Johnny's hand. He looked in the river and saw what looked like a cotton-mouth swimming away, but he wasn't sure. He went to the river's edge and scooped up a handful of mud and packed the mud around the bite on Johnny's hand.

"You bit anyplace else, Johnny? You only bit once?"

"Yeah, just on the hand, Picker. I think I got twix him and his vittles. There was a lot of frogs in them bul-rushes."

"Yo' goin' to be fine, Johnny. Cottonmouths won't kill you, but we best make camp and build us a fire. Afore this night's over, you goin' be feelin' mighty bad. But you be fine come mornin'. De mud will draw out de poison. You be a little weak from de fever is all."

"Are you sure it was a cottonmouth? You sure it wasn't a coral?" Johnny asked.

"Looked solid brown to me, Johnny. Coral's have rings on 'em."

Picker helped Johnny into a grove of cottonwoods. He hurriedly gathered wood and dry prairie grass. Re-moving Johnny's knife from his belt, he struck the dull side of the knife against the flint arrowhead. Sparks soon set the grass on fire. He then put on wood twigs until he had a good blaze. Then he put on some heavier wood. He made Johnny a bed of reeds and branches near the fire.

"You just rest now, Johnny. Ah'm goin' to make a spear out of a branch and see if Ah can catch us some fish. Ah saw some nice lookin' trout swimmin' round in dere on my way over."

"Careful in that river, Picker. It drops off mighty fast out there. Caught me by surprise."

By night fall they had dined on a trout Picker man-aged to spear. Soon Johnny was well on his way into a night of feverish delirium in which the Lords of Fate played the leading role. Picker worried but believed the poison would work its way out of his body. Johnny cried out for water from time to time and Picker had him drink as much as possible.

Dawn came with a pink gray sunrise, glimmering off the moving water and reflecting on the shimmeriing cottonwood leaves. Johnny sat up in his bed of leaves and grass and gazed upon his swollen hand. A slight movement to his right in the river drew his attention. Picker stood, knee deep in water, poised with his makeshift spear. He drew back and hurled the weapon. In seconds, he drew out a wiggling fish and walked to shore.

Johnny threw some wood on the fire. Fish for breakfast, he thought.

"You're a natural born fisherman, Picker," he said as Picker knelt down to gut and clean the fish.

"How you feelin' this mo'nin', Johnny?"

"My hand's swollen a bit, but otherwise I'm alive. Did I give you much trouble?"

"No sah, but you sho' gave de Lawds a Fate a bad time, oooowhee. Cussin' dem out somethin' awful."

"Well, I don't remember nothin' bout that, but I'm sure they deserved it."

Picker laughed a hardy laugh. Johnny looked at him with concern. "How're you feelin' Picker?"

Picker looked up from his work, with sincerity in his voice he said, "Ah'm feelin' free, Johnny." He looked around at the river and rolling prairie. "Ah'm feelin' good to be free in this country. Ah can fish and you can hunt. No need for us to go hungry. Dah Lawd is providin'."

The next day they left their camp. Staying near the river they traveled for many days. The trail became easier to follow; the wagon wheels having dug furrows in the prairie.

Soon they came upon personal belongings scattered along the trail, discarded Johnny surmised, to lighten the loads of the wagons. Tables, chairs, and an abandoned wagon. Graves also marked the trail. Markers of carved wood with the last name and hometown or state, "Roush of Illinois" and on the west bank of a creek, "Woodson of Kentucky". Just before reaching a steep bank of the river was the grave of "Ingraham of Tenn".

Johnny stopped beside this grave. "I wonder why so many graves? These people can't have been on the trail for more than two, three weeks. We've rode this trail for days, there's been no hard goin' that I can see."

"Injuns, maybe?" Picker suggested. Then walked to the abandoned wagon.

Johnny shrugged his shoulders. "I don't know, but it sure gives me the shivers. Some of those graves're fresh dug. My guess is they are the owners of that wagon," Johnny said.

"Johnny," Picker called out, "Ah found some salted bacon in dah wagon. Ah whole barrel of it, an' some water gourds, an' a map."

"Let's take what we can carry of it, Picker. Don't think these folks'll mind."

Johnny looked at the graves. With hat in hand he lowered his head. "Terribly sorry for whatever happened to you folks. I know you must've had dreams of a new life in the west, but the Lords of Fate changed all that somehow. May the Good Lord take care of you now."

Looking out across the prairie, for miles on either side of the trail before him, Johnny could see the grass had been eaten to the nub by thousands of oxen, mules, and horses that had passed before. Their defecation lay upon the trail, fouling the waters.

It suddenly occurred to Johnny that the last train to leave the frontier was Captain Manley's wagon train. They would have taken the Oregon Trail. He looked solemnly at the graves and the sullied trail. He thought of the pretty girl with the curls and of Charles William Fulbright the third. "C'mon, Picker. Let's ride," he said.

Chapter Nine

PRAIRIE STORM

The setting sun rimmed gray clouds in crimson hues and sent up rays of light like spokes in a giant wagon wheel. Slowly the sun slipped below the prairie ridge. When dusk lost its last faint glimmer of light, darkness lay oppressive on the plain. It was the time of the new moon.

Setting beside their campfire Johnny and Picker stared into the flames, their oasis of light in a sea of blackness. Johnny sat with his arms folded across his raised knees. "Wonder who they was in those graves?" he said, speaking low as if the silence of the dark prairie demanded it.

"I doin know," Picker answered through a piece of prairie grass hanging from his mouth.

A wolf howled, breaking the silence of the darkness.

"Life sure has its unexpectancies don't it? When I left Cornplanter on the Allegheny, I sure wasn't expectin' to run into so many of 'em."

"Mah mammy used to tell me that life is fulla unexpectancies and unexplainables," Picker answered. Removing the grass from his mouth, he searched the darkness at the edge of the fire light for sight or sound of the wolf.

"Yeah, my pa said as much too," Johnny agreed. "Sure wish there weren't so many so close together. A mind has trouble keepin' up with it. Tryin' to puzzle it out."

A flash of lightning lit the western darkness.

"Storm comin'. Did you hobble the horses?"

"Sho' nuff. Dey eatin' better now we got away from dah trail. Dat grass all eaten up."

Another flash. "Dat storm gettin' closer," Picker observed. "Ah wonder where dat wolf got to?"

"Yeah, I feel kind of naked out here on this plain. Not a dern tree big enough to hide under since we left the Kansas River. Wish I had a blanket," Johnny said with more than a little anxiety in his voice.

"Yup, a blanket be nice, but Ah doin need no tree if dat lightnin' get close," Picker said, picking up on Johnny's apprehension.

"Yep."

A crescendo of thunder and flashes of lightning drew closer.

"Storms sure move fast out here on the plains," Johnny observed. Peering into the darkness beyond the fire light, Johnny reassured himself. "We are just little specks out here in the grand scheme of things you know. If someone were up there in them stars lookin' down, why, they couldn't even pick us out I'll bet. So how's that fool lightin' gonna find us."

"Yup," Picker quickly agreed. "Sho' would take a passel of bad luck for dat lightnin' to git us."

Another flash and crash of thunder so close Johnny felt the ground rumble under him. "Would you say our luck has been good so far, Picker?" he asked.

"We is still alive, Johnny."

"You ain't convincin' me, Picker. I'd say we been havin' some pretty bad luck." Johnny looked at Picker across the fire. His eyes were wide and scanning the prairie.

Of a sudden, the fury of the heavens descended upon them. Lightning crashed all around in a deafening roar, lighting up the night. Rain streaked across the prairie. Johnny was up and moving fast.

"Get to the horses Picker! Hang on to 'em!" he shouted. "We can't lose the horses!"

Johnny wasn't sure Picker heard him. He could scarcely hear his own voice, but, in a flash of lightning, he saw that Picker was already hanging onto his horse's lead rope. He had his arm around his horse's neck talking into his ear.

Johnny caught up the lead rope of his mare. She was on the edge of bolting. The next crash of lightning hit close. Johnny's horse tried to raise off her forelegs, but he held her fast. She bucked her hind legs, then came off her forelegs again. This time she broke free of the hobbles. Johnny knew if he let go it would be the last he would see of her. She would run until she dropped or the storm passed, whichever came first.

During flashes of light Johnny could see Picker having the same problem with his big gelding. He was being lifted off the ground and dragged by the big horse, which had also broken its hobbles.

In the next flash Johnny could no longer see Picker. He had vanished.

The storm began to move off. Flashes of light and thunder rolled off into the distance. The crashes of lightning had been so loud that Johnny's ears rang. When he tried to holler for Picker, he could scarcely hear himself. He knew Picker would not hear him. Now the storm had moved completely across the prairie and Johnny was left deaf by the storm and blind by the darkness.

Johnny soothed his mare by rubbing and patting her, letting her know he was close by. He could hear her snorting now. The ringing in his ears subsided. The mare soon calmed down and began to graze. Johnny repaired the broken hobbles around her fetlocks and began to holler for Picker. He hollered into the darkness for the better part of an hour, but no answer came.

Johnny lay on the wet prairie floor and tried for sleep but sleep, would not come. He hollered some more, but no answer. He hoped that Picker had stopped where he was when the storm passed, rather than try to find his way back in the dark. That would cause him to wander further away. At dawn's light, he would know to move westerly but they could still miss each other by miles.

The wilderness prairie, Johnny was learning fast, is terribly unforgiving of mistakes. He thought again of the graves they had been passing for days and the abandoned wagons. Something terrible was happening. The wagon train, which wasn't big to start with, grew smaller, and consequently, more vulnerable.

·The clouds had moved off and the stars cast their faint light across the prairie. The wolves could be heard again, calling to one another. Could be they have Picker surrounded, Johnny thought.

The first light of dawn began to light the eastern sky to a gray beginning. Soon morning light gave evidence of a clear day ahead.

The sun broke over the horizon, sending glistening rays across a green, rolling prairie. Johnny scanned the vast stretch of land for Picker. Seeing no sign of him, he decided to ride north a few miles and begin a wide circle around the campsite.

Having started into the circle, heading easterly, he crested a knoll. Shading his eyes, he scanned the plain to the east. The mare sensed it first, her ears perked up and twisted forward. She whinnied, looking east. Johnny followed her gaze. There, he thought he spotted something. He strained his eyes against the sun. He saw it again, a small speck. It moved slowly and disappeared over the horizon.

Johnny made note of his position using his and the horse's shadow in relation to the campsite. He heeled the mare into a canter toward the object. Soon he saw the speck again. It was bigger and he could tell it was a horse. His mare broke into a gallop and breached the crest of another ridge.

At the bottom of the slope beyond the crest stood the gelding, drinking water from a large puddle made by the preceding storm, his rope reins dangling into the water. But no sign of Picker.

The mare sidled up to the gelding and drank from the puddle. Johnny slid off the mare. Walking slowly up to and gently talking to the gelding to sooth it, he took hold of its reins.

After drinking a bit of the water himself, Johnny crested the ridge. Looking across the prairie, he could make out the trail of Picker's horse by the impressions in the prairie grass where the stocks of grass leaned in the direction of travel. He back tracked expecting to find Picker somewhere along that trail, hurt, having been thrown from the horse.

After a few miles, he looked up from the gelding's back trail across the prairie and noticed Picker, waving his arms and jumping. Johnny heeled the mare into a full gallop, leading the gelding. When Johnny drew in rein, Picker laughed for joy.

"You lose a horse, fella?" Johnny said, excited to see Picker alive and unhurt.

"Ah sho' is happy to see you, Johnny. Ah thought, ah was lost for good. Las' night, Ah couldn't handle that big fella so Ah decided to mount him and ride him. Better dan losin' him Ah figgered. When Ah got him stopped and settled down after the storm pass, Ah din't know where Ah was, so Ah waited till mornin' and Ah rode west, but we come upon a snake, sunnin' itself in dah warm mornin' sun. Dah horse threw me an' run off. Ah was followin' his trail when Ah saw you. What a blessin' Ah swear, what a blessin'."

"Sure nuff is, Picker. I'm sure glad to see you're in one piece. You're not hurtin' anywhere are you?"

"No, Ah'm just worn from walkin' and worryin'," Picker answered.

"Well, mount up. We got to find that wagon trail agin." Johnny checked the shadow of his horse. Facing west he angled off to the southwest and the two trotted along until they came upon the washed out campfire they had the night before. They rode for several miles and picked up the wagon trail.

Many miles of prairie rolled under the horse's hooves. As they rode, they ate the dried bacon and drank from the gourds of water they found on one of the abandoned wagons. They held their mounts to a steady, easy canter so as not to tire them. Coming upon a creek they stopped. Johnny pulled the map from inside his shirt.

"This must be the Big Sandy," He surmised.

The duo crossed the creek where it flowed into the Little Blue River. When they reached the other side the two picked up the trail once again as it followed the Little Blue. They rode for days across the monotonous, tainted prairie, walking their horses, breathing in the stench of animal droppings.

They skirted around Fort Kearney, seeing no reason to let their presence be known in case word may have been received at the fort to be watchful of the fugitives, though they had long since stopped watching their back-trail.

"Don't believe that constable was the trail ridin' kind," Johnny had said, "he prefers his fancy surreys. I doubt the mate has ever set the saddle of a horse either. He's a river pirate. I don't think we have to fear them trailin' us anymore."

The landscape had changed. The green, but spindly, grasses gave way to sagebrush. The land was dry and dusty. The trail followed the south side of the Platte River for many days. The heat of the day and the rhythmic cadence of their horses had Johnny and Picker nodding off.

Suddenly the horses stopped and whinnied. Picker noticed first.

"Johnny look, someone's comin' up dah trail."

Johnny came up with a start. He shaded his eyes from the sun. "Looks to be ridin' a mule," he said.

When the rider drew close enough Johnny hollered, "Hello there!"

The man, head lowered, said nothing. He gave no indication he heard Johnny.

"I said hello there, stranger. Not very neighborly of you to . . ."

The man slowly raised his head and stared at Johnny through sunken eyes in a skeletal face. Johnny shied away.

"Geez, what's troublin' you mister? Mebbe we can help."

"Too-late-to-help-me," he mumbled haltingly. With an effort he raised his left arm and pointed a bony finger behind him.

"Help th . . ."

His arm fell to his side as he rolled off the mule. Picker slid off his horse and ran to the man now prostrate on the ground. He checked his eyes.

"He dead, Johnny," Picker reported. "Doin know why. He got no blood on him. Got to bury him best we can afore dark or dah wolves will have him. The smell of death carries far on dis heat."

Johnny, standing by his mare, looked up the trail into the rising heat and the setting sun. "Don't know what's goin' on down that trail, Picker," he said. "but I gotta feelin' we ain't gonna like whatever it is."

They lay the man out upon the ground and covered him with rocks so the wolves would not dig up the remains.

"Don't know who you were, mister," Johnny said, "but I'll trust you were a God fearin' man so I ask Him to take you to His side." He said the Lord's Prayer and ended with, "Amen."

"Amen," Picker repeated.

Johnny and Picker camped that night along the Platte River. The first signs of buffalo were their dried droppings which they used to make a campfire. There were no trees and, therefore, no wood for fire.

"What do you s'pose he was tryin' to say before he passed on?" Johnny threw the question to Picker.

"I doin know. Whatever it was it worried him to skin and bone," Picker said.

"Naw, that man died of starvation, looked to me."

"He had dried bacon in his pocket," Picker said. "I left it dere. Din't think it be good for us to eat a dead man's morsels."

"He didn't die of starvation? What then you s'pose?"

"Doin know. Mebbe he seed a ghost down dere comin' up out dah river in dah dark of night. An Injun ghost, mebbe."

Johnny looked across the fire at Picker, "You think so?" he said wide eyed. A wolf howled just outside the rim of fire light.

"Yah, Ah hear'd stories of Injun ghost down south," Picker said.

"You ever seen one?" Johnny asked.

"Naw, never see'd one. Never want to. But dat doin mean dey not out dere," Picker said, looking into the black of night for movement.

Suddenly, a scream from the darkness. A wolf caught a jackrabbit it had been stalking. Johnny and Picker both knew this, but it still bode evil in the night darkness. It proved to be a long sleepless night for both of them.

Before dawn the next morning the sudden appearance of lightning, followed shortly by rain and then by hail the size of apples, startled Johnny and Picker.

"Ouch, oww, that hurt," Johnny cried. "Get under the horses, Picker, best you can. Hang onto the lead rope."

Picker didn't respond. Johnny looked for him in the early light. Soon he heard moaning a short distance away. In searching, he nearly tripped over Picker, who was lying on the ground, covering his head.

"Ah gots hit on dah head with somethin', Johnny. Ah told you dere were ghosts out here."

"That's no ghost, Picker. That's hail. I never seen hail that size."

They tried to hide under the horses, but the horses would not stand still. When hit they would neigh, come off the ground on the hind legs and flail their forelegs in pain.

Johnny and Picker finally folded themselves into a ball and lay on the ground, protecting their heads as best they could, crying out in pain with every direct hit.

The hail storm passed and the sun cast its warming rays once again on the prairie.

"Ah hurts all over, Johnny. Like Ah was beat wit dah club."

"Yeah, me too. You got any broke bones?"

"Naw just hurtin'," Picker said.

The horses also were hurting. Not being able to complain, they hung their heads. Johnny and Picker started down the trail, limping and leading their mounts.

Two days later, the horses well enough to mount again, they came upon a mule-wagon blocking the trail. Sitting on the ground, leaning against one of the wagon wheels, wearing a wide brim hat and vest, was a young boy. His elbows resting on his up turned knees, he chewed on a blade of grass. Johnny guessed his age to be eleven or twelve. The boy seemed relieved at seeing Johnny and Picker.

"Whoa," Johnny said in shocked surprise. "Who're you?"

"Name's Mathias, Mathias Tibbs," the boy said.

"I recognize you. I saw you when Captin' Manley's wagon train left Independence," Johnny said. "What're you doin' out here all by yourself, leanin' against a wagon wheel in the middle of the prairie?" Johnny began to chuckle, seeing humor in it.

"I ain't by myself," Mathias answered. "My ma's in the wagon. Might be you come by my pa up the trail ridin' one of our mules. That what brung you here?" Mathias asked, looking sideways at Picker.

"No," Johnny answered, "we're headed to California."

Johnny indicated in the direction of the wagon. "Can we talk to yer ma?"

"Naw," Mathias replied, "she's dead. Passed on this mornin'. She'd been ailin'. Pa went back to Fort Kearney fer help. Waitin' fer him to come back so's he can say his finals and we can bury her."

Johnny shot a look at Picker. Picker looked back at him with a grim expression. Johnny hated to break the news to this boy. He wasn't sure how to go about it.

"Well, Mathias, I-I'm sure sorry 'bout your ma, I truly am. I sure hate to be the bearer of more bad news atop it, but your pa won't be comin' back."

"Oh!" Mathias exclaimed.

"He's passed on too. We buried him yesterday. He looked mighty peaked when we came upon him. Wasn't much of him left to bury. His mule ran off during the storm last night."

Mathias lowered his head. "Ma went down with the cholera," He explained. "Mustta got pa too."

"Cholera," Johnny looked at Picker, "so that's what all those graves were about back there."

"Most," Mathias said. "Some were fool accidents. One fellow shot himself with his own shotgun.

"Well, Mathias, in my way of thinkin', your ma and pa are together agin in heaven. That should give you some comfort," Johnny sympathized.

Mathias looked to the ground between his knees, spat out the grass from his mouth, then looked up at Johnny from under the brim of his hat. "Bulldung," he said.

Chapter Ten

TRYING ONE'S PATIENCE

Johnny sat his mare in stunned disbelief. He looked at Picker who gaped at Mathias.

"Bulldung!" Johnny finally exclaimed.

"Yeah, yer a nit if you believe that. Dead is dead. They're gone. Nobody knows where, but to the grave," Mathias retorted.

Exasperated Johnny said, "You gotta strange way of mournin', boy. Speakin' of the grave, we best be buryin' your ma. You gotta diggin' tool in that mule-wagon?"

"Yeah, it's down by the river. Ma always liked sittin' by the river. Said it made her feel peaceful. I started diggin' already."

"Ah doin think it's good to bury her by dah river, Mathias," Picker said. "When dah river rises it'll wash out dat grave."

"Yeah," Johnny agreed. "Let's say we dig up here, overlookin' the river, huh."

Mathias looked at Picker then at the river. "Yeah, guess yer right. That river did rise some last night," he agreed.

"Best you unhitch that mule and let him graze, Picker."

To Mathias, Johnny said, "I'm Johnny Farrell from Cornplanter on the Allegheny and this is Picker, an adventurer lookin' for riches in the west."

Mathias looked at Picker's calloused hands and muscular body. "He's a runaway slave, ya nit," he said. "What's Cornplantin' on the Allegheny got to do with anythin'?"

"No, no," Johnny explained, "that's Cornplanter, Cornplanter on the Allegheny."

"Cornplantin', geez, what a nit," Mathias said. "Come on let's git the grave dug." He shook his head, "Cornplantin' on the Allegheny. Sounds like loads of fun.

Travlin' with you two is gonna be gourds of fun I can see that. A nit and a runaway slave, geez."

Johnny looked at Picker with furrowed brow, "I believe that boy's gonna try my patience, Picker."

Picker laughed. "Ah kinda like him, he makes me chuckle," he said, walking off toward the grave site.

"Yeah, well, mebbe so but we'll dump him soon's we find a safe place!" Johnny hollered after him.

While they were digging the grave the mule Mathias' pa had been riding wondered back to join the other.

The grave completed, they interred Mrs. Tibbs. Mathias looked the other way as Johnny and Picker filled the grave with dirt. Johnny said the Lord's Prayer over her resting place above the river. Johnny thought it a rather nice place for the gravesite. Picker fashioned a wooden cross and asked Johnny to write the epitaph. "Ah doin know writin'," Picker said.

Johnny ask Mathias if there was anything special he wanted written on the cross. Mathias, still standing over the grave, circling the brim of his hat around in his hand, shrugged his shoulders.

· "I don't know," he said softly, "Mebbe . . . I don't know . . ."

"Mebbe what, Mathias?" Johnny asked.

"Mebbe, 'I lov . . . ,' I don't know!" he shouted and walked hurriedly back to the wagon.

Johnny looked at Picker who was twisting the brim of his hat in his hand. Picker nodded his head and turned toward the wagon.

"Gots to hook up dah team," he said as he walked away.

Johnny withdrew his knife, sat down and started to carve.

The mule-wagon, wheel hubs squeaking, moved slowly across the prairie with Johnny and Picker riding beside it.

Several miles back on the trail a wooden cross stood at the head of a grave overlooking the river. On the cross was roughly carved, "I love you mother July 1852."

*****

The miles were measured in days and then weeks. The prairie had become a panorama of suffocating heat and dry landscape. If it weren't for the Platte River nearby travel would have been near impossible. The boys stopped, from time to time, to water the animals and douse their hats in the river, placing them on their heads to keep them cool. They dreamed of the last cool rain a few weeks back.

Mathias urged his mules, Dan and Dave, along the dusty trail.

"Picker!" Johnny yelled from further up the trail. "I'm gonna go scout ahead so we don't run headlong into any trouble! Just keep following the trail. I'll be back inna few hours!"

To Mathias he said, "best you grease those hubs, Mathias, or you'll be walkin' soon! I hear'em clear over here!"

"Yes, captin'!" Mathias answered, "right away, captin' sir!"

Picker nodded with a smile.

Johnny looked toward Mathias and shook his head. "That boy sure grates on me," he said to himself, then rode out.

The prairie rolled and swelled mile after mile like an ocean frozen in time. Nothing was in sight in all those miles, but Johnny had the feeling he was being watched. Each time he approached a swell, he dismounted and walk cautiously up the swell to peer over it before continuing on.

He stopped at a creek bordered by small cottonwoods and dismounted. He knelt down to drink of the water. He noticed a hoof print in the mud at the edge of the water. The print was fresh and, he noted, unshod.

Looking around, he saw more prints along the edge of the stream. Indians, he thought. He guessed there must have been at least eight or ten ponies watering there only a few minutes before.

Fear swept through his body as he slowly rose to his feet. He looked behind him, but saw nothing.

The mare showed no awareness of ponies close by. Johnny was sure she would be the first to sound the alarm. When the mare finished her drink, he mounted and casually ascended the bank of the creek and noticed the unshod prints heading north away from the wagon trail.

Must have just missed them, he thought. What good fortune. Who's to say they were hostile, but who wants to find out?

Johnny suddenly had a terrible feeling that the Indians may have turned to the east. If so, they would see Mathias' wagon. He rode hard back down the trail.

Picker and Mathias were moving slowly up the trail when Johnny crested a swell and saw them. He rode up to the pair and slid to a stop.

"Indians," he shouted. "I saw fresh, unshod prints goin' north. I almost run headlong into them. I think we should make cold camp tonight, no fire. No use invitin' trouble."

"Looks like 'nother storm comin', Johnny," Picker pointed out, "a fire be no use anyways."

Johnny looked to the southwest where Picker had indicated. He saw a distant cloud forming. "Yeah, let's make camp here. Mathias you're gonna have company in that wagon tonight. I ain't sleepin' on no wet ground, gettin' pelted by hail while we have that wagon for shelter. That storm's probably 'nother fast mover anyhow."

They unhitched the mules and hobbled them, then hobbled the horses. They secured the canvas cover, closed the end openings of the wagon, then settled down to wait out the storm.

Except for the glow of the light of day through the canvas and light coming through the small end openings, the interior of the wagon was dark.

"How you two come to be travlin' together?" Mathias asked.

"Well," Johnny explained, "we met on a riverboat out of Pittsburgh." Johnny went on to explain how he had rafted down the Allegheny River after his father's death and found himself aboard the *Mary Louise* from which Picker was in the process of escaping.

He described their escape and the demise of the *Mary Louise* at Westport and their close call with the constable and the mate. "Been ridin' west ever since," Johnny concluded.

"Yer pa has passed on too?" Mathias asked.

"Yeh," Johnny said, "He was kilt early spring this year."

"How so?" Mathias asked.

"My pa was the lead raftsman on the Allegheny," Johnny explained. "The way it was told to me by the survivors, they were poling a train of hardwood log rafts from the upper Allegheny bound for mills in Pittsburgh. A heavy spring rain came after a week of heavy snowfall. The ice was jammed and piled high along the banks of the river. When the ice began to break free, Pa did his best to maneuver the rafts, but the heavy rain blinded him. The lead raft started into a free spin, went out of control and rammed a solid chunk of ice. It threw my pa into the water where he was caught between the ice block and the second raft." Johnny shivered and paused, thinking about it again.

They sat in the covered wagon engrossed in Johnny's story as the wind picked up outside.

Johnny continued. "The lumber mill company gave me Pa's last wages so I figured I would buy me passage on a riverboat and head west to the gold fields."

"So you got money, huh?" Mathias asked.

"Nope, I lost it all in the Allegheny River when I dang near drowned," Johnny grimaced at the memory, "or someone on the *Mary Louise* stole it."

"So here you are, sittin' out here on the prairie, penniless, wanted by the law with a runaway slave as a partner. I'd say from where I'm sittin' ya look like a dern loser. What a nit."

"Who're you to talk? You're settin' here too," Johnny retorted.

"It twern't my fault I'm here," Mathias shot back. "I dint want to leave Illinois. Ma didn't either. We tried to tell Pa but he had his mind made up. I told Ma to let Pa go if he was all tarnation set on it, I would run the farm myself, but no, she said it was her duty to go with Pa. She shoulda listened to me; she'd still be alive."

"Who's to say she wouldn't of come down with the ailment in Illinois and passed on anyways," Johnny suggested.

"Bulldung, she had cholera. Ain't no cholera in Illinois."

"Seems to me," Johnny went on, "there ain't no sense to sittin' here frettin' about what was or shoulda been. The question at hand is what you do from here on. You can't be blamin' your folks for your perdicament. I'm sure they did what they thought was best at the time."

"They didn't do what was best fer me, that's sure," Mathias argued, "an' I ain't got the slightest notion what I'm gonna do from here on."

They were quiet in the darkness for a while, then Johnny heard Mathias mumble, "Gotta find a way to make fast money."

"Sure," Johnny said, "tie in with me an' Picker and go to California to find gold."

"Nah, you nit, that sounds too much like work. You have to dig for that stuff you know. I hope you ain't been taken by the stories about it layin' top the ground," Mathias said, looking sideways at Johnny in the dark.

"W-Well," Johnny stammered.

"Geez," Mathias teased, "you have, ain't you? What a idjit."

"No, I ain't no idjit neither," Johnny insisted, "and I don't believe it's just layin' on the ground to pickup. Picker and me ain't afraid of work. Huh Picker?"

Johnny directed his question in the direction he thought Picker to be sitting in the darkness of the wagon, but no answer came.

"Picker!"

"I do believe you put him to sleep," Mathias said through a yawn, "I'm sleepy myself. Yer jawin's enough to put a body to sleep."

"Just the same," Johnny felt his anger rising, "we ain't afraid of a little work and a little work wouldn't hurt you any either. Might make a friendlier person of you. Always whinin' and complainin'. And I ain't no nit so you can quit callin' me that."

Mathias mumbled in the darkness, "Geez, look who's talkin' 'bout whinin' and complainin'. Yer enough to wake the dead."

"Hah," Johnny retorted, "you just said my jawin' was enough to put a body to sleep. Now you're sayin' I'll wake the dead. You don't know what you're talkin' bout, do you?"

Signaling the others with his right hand raised Picker whispered, "What's dat?"

"What? I don't hear nothin'," Mathias whispered.

"Yeah, that's the trouble," Johnny whispered. Sensing the air, he said, "No, locust, no birds, no nothin'. Too quiet."

They looked at one another for answers, listening, but no sound or answers came.

Johnny moved his hand and laid it on the handle of his knife. He eased over to the end cover and slowly began to untie the draw rope.

"Listen," Mathias said, "Hear that?"

His eyes widening in the half light, Picker said, "Ah hears it."

A low roar met Johnny's ears. Peering out through the hole in the end opening he saw a strange orange glow where once there was daylight. He swiftly crawled over Mathias and Picker to the other end of the wagon and drew open the end flap and gasped at what he saw.

For a few seconds he was unable to form words upon his lips or get them to come out.

Impatient, Mathias hollered, "What? What?"

Johnny turned to Picker and Mathias and pointed out the canvas opening. "T-tor-tornado!" he stammered.

The roar soon became a rumbling, frightening siege upon the prairie as it moved and twisted toward the wagon. Winds picked up. Sand and dust blew through the canvas openings. Johnny tried to muster his mind into deciding the safest course of action, but the screaming winds bore down upon them. There was nothing to do but hang onto the wagon sides and pray, which came out in screams from all three.

The wagon rocked from side to side. The canvas top strained against the iron hoops and finally tore at the seams. Suddenly, Johnny felt the wagon itself lifting off the ground. It settled back down on its wheels, then lifted again.

The canvas gave way and flew off into the darkness of sand and dust. The boys covered their faces from the sand and laid down in the bottom of the wagon, gasping for air that seemed to have been taken away with the canvas top.

The wagon lifted off the ground again. It floated, gently rocking. The thinning of the air within the wagon caused Johnny to slip away into a dreamy world of slumber. "Floating," he thought, "like on the raft in the river. It makes me sleepy, so sleepy. The sound of the moving river splashing against the sides of the raft, rocking it, rocking me to sleep."

"Yes, Johnny," a voice said. "Go to sleep. You are very sleepy. I'll rock the boat for you. I'll rock you to sleep."

"Boat?" Johnny dreamed. "But I'm not on a boat, I'm on a raft. Who're you, nit, that you don't know the difference?   Anybody knows a raft has wheels and is drawn by mules and floats."

Ah, 'tis the Lords of Fate I see, come to do me harm, but no harm shall come to me as, now, I set upon the prairie."

"Floats?" Johnny sat straight up in the wagon. "I'm dreamin'! Rafts don't have wheels! Wagons don't float!"

A loud crash and hard jolt threw Johnny face down in the sand of the prairie. The wagon, laying on its side, loomed over him. The wind passed on.

Picker screamed in pain.

Looking to his left Johnny saw Picker, his left arm pinned under one of the iron hoops. "Johnny!" Picker screamed, "Help me!"

Johnny looked around for Mathias. "Mathias, where are you?"

"Over here," he answered.

"You hurt?"

"No, don't think so."

"Get the mules, we got to pull this wagon off Picker."

Picker hollered in pain again.

"I can't see hide nor hair of the mules. They're gone!" Mathias had climbed to the top of the ravine.

"Come here then and help me! Hurry!"

Mathias scrambled down the slope. "Get ready to pull Picker out from under this hoop. I'm going to try to raise it."

"Hang tight, Picker," Mathias said. "I know you're hurtin'."

Johnny pulled up on the hoop, straining. He released the pressure from Picker's arm just enough for Picker, with Mathias' help, to slide out from under it. Johnny released the hoop and fell backward.

"Is it broke?" Johnny asked, coming over to Picker.

"Naw," Picker said, gasping in pain. "Ah doin' think so. Sho' hurts, but Ah kin bend it."

Johnny grabbed a tattered piece of canvas remnant from the wagon and made Picker a sling. "You're gonna be resting for a few days, Picker. No heavy work for you."

"Ahh, Ah'm doin' just fine now," he said.

Wide eyed, Johnny searched the eerie orange glow. The wind calmed to a moan in the distance. Dusk settled upon them. The animals had vanished. Discouraged. Johnny thought, stranded on this God forsaken endless prairie, miles from who knows where.

Chapter Eleven

A PROMISE MADE

In the faint light of dawn the next morning the three walked up the embankment and scanned the prairie, but saw nothing of the mules or horses.

"Best we separate and search in three different directions," Johnny suggested. "Odds are in our favor. We'll meet back here at the wagon when the sun is a quarter past sunrise with or without the mules and horses. Take some jerky along for breakfast and a canteen of water. You gonna be all right, Picker?"

Picker was still a little befuddled by the events of the night before. "Ah doin' know how all dat wind come so suddent," he said, shaking and scratching his head with hat in hand.

"Well, Picker," Mathias said. "You're lucky to be alive I reckon."

Looking at the overturned wagon and their scattered belongings, Johnny said, "The way I see it that tornado blew past us for the most part. Else that wagon would have been splinters and we would have been full of them. We got the Lord to thank again."

"Oh, there you go again, singin' yer biblical praises," Mathias groaned.

"You head north, Mathias," Johnny directed. "I'll be glad to be away from yer complainin' for awhile. You know which direction is north?"

"Course I do," Mathias answered.

"I'll head west, Picker. I'll see if I can pickup the trail again. Keep an eye out for signs of the trail, Mathias. Those wagon ruts should show up pretty plain. Most likely you will be the first to cross it."

"Yes sir, captin," Mathias mocked, getting in a parting shot as he walked away.

"Mathias," Johnny said with a wry smile, "that ain't north if the rising sun's on yer left."

"Ahhh, I know it ain't, just goin' down here to blow wind," Mathias lied, lifting his leg at Johnny.

"We had nuff wind, Mathias," Picker joked.

Johnny and Picker smiled at each other. "You seed the Lawds of Fate las' night, Johnny?" Picker asked.

"Yep, sure did at that," Johnny answered.

"What dey say?" Picker asked.

"Not much. They just tried to make me sleep. I'll just bet they were about to send that wagon on a flyin' trip and kill us all three. Don't tell Mathias about the Lords of Fate. He'll just make a fuss about it and I don't want to hear it. See you in awhile, Picker, keep a skinned eye for the animals. They may be close by and come wandering back. I tie their hobbles in a slip knot at night so's they don't break their legs if somethin' startles 'em. Pray we find them, we for sure need 'em."

"Sho nuff, Johnny. Sho hope ah never sees dem Lawds of Fate," Picker said.

The rising sun warmed Johnny's back as he walked west scanning the horizon for movement. Gonna be a hot day, he thought.

A few hours into his search Johnny had seen neither trace nor track of the mules and horses. The sun near quarter past rising, he sat down on a rise where he could see for miles in all directions. He removed a piece of jerky from his pack.

Chewing on the jerky, Johnny gazed across the prairie. He tried to imagine how they could continue on without the mules and horses. They need the supplies that are on the wagon and the wagon itself for shelter, but most of all, walking the rest of the way would slow them down. If someone were following them--which was never too far from Johnny's mind--they could over take them easily even if they were driving a carriage.

"We need those animals," Johnny said, scanning the horizon once more before backtracking himself to the wagon. Mathias or Picker may have found them by now, he thought. Pray to God they did.

When Johnny returned to the wagon, he found Picker clearing the brush and sand from around the wagon. It looked to Johnny like he was preparing to hitch the mules though he saw no mules around.

"Have you found the mules, Picker?" he asked.

"Naw, Johnny. Just thought Ah'd git the wagon ready for when one of you came along wit dem we can set dis wagon upright."

"Mathias hasn't returned yet?"

"Nope, ah gettin' worried 'bout him now. Been gone too long. He not too good wit directions."

"Yeah, maybe I shoulda had him stay here, but you know as well as I, he would have put up a fuss 'bout that."

"Sho' nuff he would of," Picker agreed.

"That sun's almost straight overhead. Gettin' hot out on that prairie," Johnny worried. "He's out there wonderin' around in circles no doubt. Best I be goin' out to find him."

"You want me to go wit ya, Johnny?" Picker asked.

"Naw, best you stay here in case he returns, Picker. You're doin' a good job of diggin' that wagon out. Sure hope you ain't doin' it for nothin'. How's your arm?"

"It hurt bad, Johnny, but I think it be better soon."

Johnny started out going north, trying to follow Mathias' trail, but in the dried and parched terrain, the trail was hard to see. He decided to walk due north, keeping his eyes skinned left and right. He was sure Mathias fell into a wide arch as he walked and may even be headed back toward the wagon or missed it altogether.

He could be anywhere, Johnny thought, or worse... Johnny's breath caught in his throat, . . . or worse he may have fell prey to those Indians I saw signs of. I hope they're friendly. Sure they must be friendly, there ain't been any Indian trouble in years, 'course the ol' man back in Independence did say there has been some Indian attacks on wagons lately.

Johnny stopped and scanned the horizon again, shielding his eyes. He mumbled to himself. "That sure would be awful if Mathias met an untimely end. I sure wish I would've been more patient with him. I feel awful I got mad at him, but darned he can be a peezer. Naw, he ain't that bad. I just got me a temper. I get to regrettin' that temper. Lord, you bring Mathias and those animals back safe and I promise I will never get mad at Mathias again. After all, he is just an orphan."

Johnny eyes began to mist. "Yeah, he lost his ma and pa almost on the same day. He's just sufferin' the loss of his folks a little different than most folks do. I remember gettin' angry when Ma passed on. It didn't seem fair to me. I got angry but didn't know who to be angry at. Yeah, I remember that and I wasn't but Mathias' age. Why didn't I understand that? I could have been more patient. Now I may not have the chance. I may never see Mathias alive again. Please Lord, don't let me come upon his lifeless body out here. I'll never forgive myself."

Once again Johnny stopped to scan the horizon, but everything looked blurry. He wiped across his eyes with the back of his dusty shirt sleeve and looked again. He saw something moving far off. He strained through misty eyes and the shimmering of heat on the prairie. He saw forms now, standing still.

"Rocks, mebbe?" he guessed.

"Antelope? Darn!" he shouted.

Moving again, there appeared to Johnny to be three of them. "No four, six, eight," he counted. "They're gettin closer. Wish I had my shotgun, I sure would like a bit of fresh meat for a change."

Johnny's eyes cleared just then. Out of the rising heat, he watched them approach. "Whoa," he said. "Those're horses . . . and riders, and . . . Indians?"

Johnny froze in his steps, a shot of fear coursed through his body. He heard his heart pounding in his ears. Then he saw him, riding behind the Indians mounted on a mule, waving. It was Mathias. Johnny forgot any fear he had and took off in a bounding run toward the mounted Indians, ready to do battle. He never gave a second thought to the fact that he wasn't armed. "Mathias!" he shouted.

Mathias put the mule in a canter. Coming around the Indians, he reached Johnny first and slid off the mule.

"Hey Johnny, I got the horses an' mules. The Indians helped me round them up. Had a wezzle of a time out here."

Johnny ground to a halt in front of Mathias. He saw that the Indians were holding back.

"What the . . . ?" He said no more and hugged Mathias. "I feared you was hurt or dead out here."

"I likely coulda been if it weren't for them Pawnee. I was plum lost. This dang prairie looks the same in all directions, I swear."

"Mathias, you did great my boy, just great," Johnny lauded.

The Indians turned their ponies and rode off toward the northwest. One of them stopped just as the others disappeared over a rise. He turned and raised his arm in a wave. Mathias waved back. The Indian turned and disappeared over the rise.

"That was young Two Hawks," Mathias said. "I liked him. He was the only one who could speak a little English. He said we should be watchful of the Sioux. We are entering their range and they are becoming hostile. He said the Sioux would have scalped me, took the horses and ate the mules."

"You're a mighty lucky boy, Mathias. Thank God for your deliverance this day!"

Johnny swung onto his horse and took up the lead rope of Picker's horse. "Hey," he said, "the Indians give you these ropes? They're mighty fine ropes. Look to be made from horse hair."

"Yep," Mathias said. Then he noticed Johnny's face. "Your eyes are dirty, like you been cryin' or somethin'. You been cryin', Johnny? You worry 'bout me that much?"

"Course I ain't been cryin', what're you thinkin', boy?"

Johnny heeled his mount out ahead of Mathias. He felt his temper begin to flare.

"I'm thinkin' you been cryin', that's what I'm thinkin'. You been wipin' yer eyes and nose on yer sleeve too, huh? Just like a dern baby. Wait'll I tell Picker." Mathias took to song, "Johnny's been cryin', Johnny's been cryin'"

Johnny looked to the heavens and mumbled, "Yes Lord, I remember my promise."

"Oh, yeah that reminds me," Mathias said, having heard a little of Johnny's mumbling, "tell me 'bout them Lords of Fate you was tellin' Picker 'bout this mornin'. You seein' bogy men in yer dreams, Johnny? The Looorrrds of Fate, Scar-ry."

Johnny looked to the heavens again, "You findin' this humorous, Lord?" he asked.

Chapter Twelve

THE GIFT

The endless prairie of dust, sagebrush, and heat stretched before them. Lizards scurried about, leaving wiggly trails in the sand to be blown asunder by the hot desert wind.

Johnny did his best to ignore Mathias and eventually Mathias got quiet. Must've give up 'cause he couldn't get to me. Gonna have to remember that, he thought.

The heat shimmered above the dust and sage bringing a thirst to Johnny's parched throat. He stopped to take a pull from his canteen. Thinking Mathias was awfully quiet of a sudden, Johnny turned to make sure Mathias was still behind him. Mathias regarded him with a thoughtful look and a pleasant smile, but said nothing.

"Somethin' wrong, Mathias?" Johnny asked.

"No, Johnny. Everything's fine," Mathias replied.

"Hmmm, yer awfully quiet. Not that I miss yer hecklin'. Sure you ain't ailin' er somethin'?"

"Nope, just fine," Mathias repeated. Johnny turned and heeled his mare to a walk again.

Presently Mathias heeled his mule up beside Johnny. "Was you really worried bout me, Johnny?" he asked.

"Aaah, I was wonderin' how long it would take for you to start again," Johnny said. "You've had your fun, Mathias. Give it up."

"I'm sorry fer hecklin' you, Johnny."

"Yeah, sure." Johnny replied with doubt.

"No, I mean it," Mathias assured him.

Coming over a rise they saw Picker standing by the wagon. "There's Picker," Johnny said. "Let's get those mules hitched up. We can journey a few miles before dark."

Johnny waved at Picker and picked up the pace, leading Picker's gelding. Picker waved back, jumping up and down, waving his hat in jubilation. Johnny and Mathias reined up and dismounted.

"Ah sho' am happy to see you two," Picker laughed with joy and slapped both Johnny and Mathias on their backs.

"We're happy and, I must add, lucky to be back," Johnny said, with a glance at Mathias.

After they got the wagon back on its wheels and the mules hitched up Mathias told the story of his encounter with the Pawnee Indians. Nodding toward the mules and horses Mathias said, "I found those ornery critters only a few miles from here, but I couldn't get them rounded up. They kept runnin' off, gettin' further away from the wagon. My guess is they was still skittish from the storm. Then outta nowhere comes these Indians. I was scared. Thought I was a goner fer sure. They rounded up the critters and put lead ropes on 'em. I figgered they just wanted the horses and mules and would not harm me, but then they led the animals up and handed the ropes to me so's I could lead them back. They knew what I was up to. They have been following us for days."

"Mustta been the tracks I saw," Johnny surmised.

Picker listened intently while hitching up the mules to the wagon. "Sho' am happy dere friendly," he said.

"Trouble is," Johnny said, "we will soon be entering Sioux territory."

"Yeah," Mathias continued, "the Pawnee say the Sioux are roaming in war parties. They say the white man is over-grazing the prairie, killing too many buffalo. They kill for fun and leave the carcass to rot on the prairie. The tribes need the buffalo to survive. The Pawnee fear we're in danger, being lone trav'lers and easy prey for robbing."

"So," Johnny advised, "we are gonna have to be extra watchful. From now on no campfires after dark. We make cookfires in daylight and put them dead out before dusk."

Picker's joy was short lived. "What we gonna do if dah Sioux come?" he asked.

"I don't know, Picker. Throw stones at'em I 'spose," Johnny said, discouraged at their lack of defense.

"Johnny, I got somethin' for you." Mathias reached behind him and opened a door under the wagon bench. He pulled out a rifle encased in a buckskin scabbard.

Johnny's mouth dropped open. "You had that under the seat all along? Why didn't you bring it out b'fore this? We coulda been eatin' antelope steaks," he said.

"I didn't know that one of you might have stole it from me, or shot me with it. It was my protection just in case. Here. I'm giving it to you." He handed it down to Johnny.

"Wait a minute," Johnny said, "yer givin' it to me?"

"Yeah. You know how to load an' shoot it?"

"Sure do," Johnny said removing the scabbard. "Wow, it's a fifty caliber Hawkens Plains rifle. Was this yer pa's?"

"Yep, my grandpappy was a trapper. Gave it to my pa when the trappin' business went belly-up. Grandpappy was too old for trappin' anyhow."

"I can't accept this, Mathias," Johnny explained. "This has been handed down in your family and someday you can give it to a son of yours. B'sides, you still may need it for protection where we're headed."

"I still got protection," Mathias said. He reached inside his vest pocket and pulled out a very small hand gun.

"A Derringer!" Johnny exclaimed. "You sure needed a lot of protection from me and Picker. Do we look that dangerous? That was your grandpappy's too?"

"Nope, that was my ma's. Pa gave it to her for protection to keep on her person at all times. I keep it in my vest pocket. Primed and ready. Real handy, you know."

"Yeah, I see." Johnny shot a look at Picker. "Tell you what Mathias I can't accept ownership of this rifle, much as I'd like to, but, I'm a fair shot. I'll use it to feed and protect us while we travel together. I'll take good care of it for you. Do you have ball, powder and wads?"

"Yep," Mathias said, "An' caps too. Things're kinda tossed all over in the bench compartment, but I'll get it sorted out. " He leaned behind the bench and, almost standing on his head, rooted around and came up with a powder horn and pouch of four forty balls.

"You know how to shoot a rifle, Picker?" Johnny asked.

"No Ah doin knows how. Never did have one in mah hands. Dey makes a lotta noise is all Ah knows."

"Let me show you how to load first," Johnny said. "That takes some knowin'. Then I'll show you how to aim and shoot. Best you know how to shoot. May come a time on this journey when it will save your life. Just re-member--powder, patch, ball n' cap in that order. Pow-der, patch, ball n' cap. Get them outta order and it won't fire. Put too much of either in or not ram them down proper, when you pull that trigger it'll sure's hell get your attention. If you don't put the cap in, 'course it won't fire at all."

"First, you have to make the wad moist either with grease or spit. Since we have little grease and plenty of spit, spit it is. You take the wad and put it in your mouth to make it wet, while you pour a measure of powder down the barrel. Oh, say . . . this much," Johnny said as he poured then stopped.

"Then you take the wad from your mouth and place it over the muzzle and place a ball on the wad and push it in a little. Then you take the rod and push the ball and wad down the barrel, like this. Then tap the ball with the rod until the rod bounces. You gotta have that ball and wad firmly into the powder. If there is a gap there, it could breach on you."

"What you mean, breach?" Picker asked.

"Blow up!" Johnny answered.

"Oh, oh," Picker said.

"There," Johnny said after placing the percussion cap on the hammer nipple. "Now we are loaded for bear, or anything else. What you want to do is always keep a wad wet an' ready for reloadin' in case you miss the first time, you can reload and fire again. A good woodsman, like the one who taught me, can load a Hawkens quicker than you can think about it. I keep a wad in each cheek when I'm huntin' big game an' caps at my finger tips."

"There's more powder in the wagon, Johnny, but you got all the lead ball we own in that pouch."

"You gotta bullet mold in that wagon, Mathias?" Johnny asked.

"Yeah, sure, but we got no lead."

"We got lead right here," Johnny said, holding up the pouch.

"What good dat do. When you shoot it, it gone for good," Picker observed.

"Yeah," Mathias agreed.

"Well, seems I got to tell you boys a story. I know'd of a man back in Pennsylvania who shot nine deer with one lead ball. So there's no reason why we can't shoot nine targets with one lead ball."

"Nine deer! That's not poss'ble," Mathias argued.

"Sure 'tis, Mathias," Johnny said, "you think on that tonight and I'll show you how it's done come the morrow."

"I sincerely give you that rifle fer concernin' yerself so out there on the prairie, Johnny," Mathias said.

Johnny regarded Mathias thoughtfully, then quietly he said, "That's mighty kind of you, Mathias. You ready to roll that wagon now?"

"Yep, sure am," Mathias said happily.

"We soon oughtta be coming upon the South Platte," Johnny said, examining the map he pulled from inside his shirt. Scanning the prairie he said, "Keep that wagon on the trail, Mathias, and holler if you see trouble comin'. Let's keep a watch on our back trail, Picker. Best we see trouble before it sees us."

"What we do if trouble come, Johnny?" Picker asked.

"We do what trouble makes us do, Picker," Johnny said. Evading the obvious in Picker's question, he added, "Nothing more, nothing less."

Johnny was troubled by Picker's question. Indeed, what would they do if trouble came in the form of an Indian war party?

The three of them moved across the vast prairie in slow procession. Mathias stayed close to Johnny when he wasn't driving the mules. At times he talked Picker into driving the wagon so he could ride Picker's gelding along with Johnny.

Occasionally, Johnny shot an antelope for camp meat. He proudly and protectively carried the rifle in one hand across the mare's withers, feeling a little more safe having it. He knew, however, if the Sioux came riding down on them he would have little chance for defense. Shooting then reloading a muzzle loader took time. Their only hope was to somehow make the Sioux think them stronger than they actually were if the time should come. He sincerely hoped and prayed it would not.

The marked graves along the trail gave Johnny reason to believe trouble and death could be just a thought away.

Chapter Thirteen

THE STAMPEDE

High over the Platte River within view of the group moving across the sultry prairie, a hawk soars. Suddenly it flapped its wings, held its course a moment, then, in a swift motion of natural grace, dipped its wing and dove away toward the southwest.

Riding out ahead of Picker and Mathias, Johnny's attention had been drawn to the hawk when its shadow passed in front of him. When it flew off to the southwest, he reflected on the idea that it may have seen something on their back trail it did not like. He wished he could see through the eyes of the hawk for he had become wary of the dangers of the prairie and was becoming sensitive to anything out of the ordinary. "I'm gettin' jumpy," he mumbled.

Johnny raised his arm for the others to stop. He wasn't sure yet why he wanted to stop and didn't know what to tell Picker when he rode up beside him.

"What's wrong, Johnny?" Picker asked.

"Don't know," Johnny said. He looked toward the southwest where the hawk had flown. "Don't know for sure."

Their horse's ears twisted forward then back. Their heads raised, turned, and looked back intently.

The animals became restive.

"Ah hears somethin', Johnny," Picker straightened up on his horse--listening.

"You sure have good hearing, Picker," Johnny said as he followed the horses gaze behind them. "I don't hear nothin' unusual . . . wait, what's that?" Johnny pointed where a cloud was hovering. "That ain't no storm cloud, looks like dust, like a high wind is blowing up. What do you hear, Picker?"

"Sounds like dah roar of dat tornado," Picker dismounted. "Dis time ah feels it in the ground?"

Johnny looked for a ravine or wallow to use for cover, but the prairie afforded no such protection. The horses were becoming difficult to hold. Johnny looked back and saw that Mathias was having trouble holding the mules back.

"Get those mules under control Mathias!" Johnny ordered.

"I'm tryin'," were the last words Johnny heard from Mathias as the mules bolted.

"Come on, Picker," Johnny yelled, "We have a runaway wagon on our hands."

What the hawk had seen and the three boys would soon encounter was a phalanx of buffalo in a stampede across the parched prairie, spooked by some unknown force. Throwing up dust high onto the air currents, the buffalo ran headlong, dodging left and right. With no particular leader to guide on, they ran at a pounding roar to the west in a head-on course toward the lone wagon miles ahead.

Johnny and Picker flanked the wagon. Riding up on either side of the mules they grasped the halters of both mules and forced them to a halt. The mules were wide-eyed and difficult to restrain. Johnny turned and saw the reason for their terror.

Moving along the vast expanse of the horizon, heads lowered, the buffalo thundered under a cloud of dust. Johnny searched for a break in the line of woolly monsters bearing down on them. Something familiar in him took over. He recognized it as the force that got him through the perils of the Allegheny, the *Mary Louise*, and escaping the law in Independence; it was simply the instinct of survival. He began to shout orders.

"Let the mules go, Picker! Hang onto those reins, Mathias! Your only hope is to keep that wagon upright and the mules controlled as best you can! Turn them when I give the orders!"

To Picker he yelled, "We've got to find a break in the line to ease into and run with them best we can!"

The mules broke out at a run as the buffalo approached. Johnny was captivated by the size of the herd and the immensity of the animals.

"Dere, Johnny!" Picker shouted. He reined his gelding around to the north, pointing toward a section of the herd that was thinning out. The buffalo were bunching up to the south.

"Turn that wagon northward, Mathias!" Johnny shouted. Mathias didn't hear him. The bawling and thundering noise of the herd made Johnny's shout seem a mere whisper. He rode hard to the right side of the wagon. Seizing Dan's halter, he heeled and reined his mare hard to the right. The wagon made the hard turn after tilting slightly and Mathias, stiffened with fear, grasped the bench to keep from going over the side.

They were now in the middle of the bellowing, roaring herd moving west. In the thickening dust Johnny lost sight of Picker, but held fast to the mule's halter. He knew the buffalo were capable of capsizing the wagon if they crashed into it broadside. The only way out, he thought, was to move with the herd and ease off. The herd was still miles deep and mostly behind them. The dust was stifling. It caked into mud on Johnny's sweating neck and forehead and gritted in his teeth. He unbuttoned his shirt and brought it up around his nose and mouth.

The enormous animals buffeted Johnny's mare. Her ears drawn back and nostrils flared, she eyed the buffalo. Swinging her long neck she butted the animals with her head as she ran. Johnny's greatest fear now was that she might be gored by the horns of one of the mighty beasts, but as he looked around he saw only young ones in the immediate area. Still, he kept a wary watch.

Suddenly, out of the dust, Picker appeared. His big gelding seemingly undaunted by the gigantic buffalo. Stepping sideways in a canter, he sidled up to Johnny's mare coming between her and the herd. That gelding's been among buffalo before, Johnny thought.

Johnny let his shirt fall and signaled Picker in approval and brought his shirt back up around his nose and mouth. Picker, seeing the merits of that, did the same with his shirt.

Just as Johnny convinced himself they were going to survive this new ordeal, Picker tapped him on the shoulder and pointed toward the wagon. Johnny turned around and saw that Mathias was missing.

Johnny groaned in despair. Had he turned the wagon too quickly for Mathias to recover? Was Mathias lying out there on the prairie being trampled into the dust by thousands of buffalo? Those thoughts brought him to near panic. He glanced at Picker whose brow was furrowed with question and concern. Johnny guessed he had the same thoughts.

"Take hold this mule, Picker!" Johnny shouted, motioning toward the halter. Picker sidled up next to the mule as Johnny eased back along the reigns until he was alongside the wagon bench.

He raised up on his horse, peering into the wagon. "Mathias!" Johnny called, hearing no answer. Johnny noted the reins were not dragging along the ground where he would have expected them to be had they been dropped. Seeing that the reins were lying across the bench and into the wagon, Johnny called again, "Mathias?" Then he saw a hand coming up from below the bench. It waved then went back down quickly, then the other hand came up holding the reins firmly.

Johnny burst into laughter in spite of the situation. He rode back to Picker and motioned for him to turn around. Picker, upon seeing the raised hand full of reins behind the bench, burst into laughter.

"I told him to hang onto those reins!" Johnny shouted in laughter.

The last of the herd moved past them now, turning to the south. The dust began to thin out and breathing became easier. They stopped the wagon. When the dust finally settled they saw why the herd had turned. The buffalo had run up against a river and were following its course south or splashing into the water.

"Yahoo!" Johnny shouted. "We're safe now! They've tuckered themselves out!"

"Dey was stampedin' to water," Picker agreed.

Mathias, crawling out from under the bench of the wagon, complained, "Yeah, and dern near killed us doin' it."

"Well dang," Johnny chided Mathias. "There's Mathias. You have an enjoyable ride in there, boy?"

"You dern near lost me when you made that turn back there. I figured if you weren't gonna let me drive the wagon I'd just get inside and hang on," Mathias explained.

"Hah, if you'd drove that wagon from where you were hidin' you'd be back in Saint Louie by now." Johnny and Picker laughed.

"You sho' had us scared, Mathias. We thoughts you gone and fell off dat wagon."

·   "I dern near did," Mathias grumbled.

"In the whole scheme of things out here on this prairie we don't mean much more to them beasts then a herd of turtles. They'd of stomped us into the dust and wouldn't have missed a step. That's a mighty animal," Johnny said in admiration. He removed · the map from inside his shirt and followed the markings. He then handed it to Picker.

"Looks to me like we just run up against the South Platte crossing. Wouldn't you agree, Picker?"

"Yup," Picker agreed. "An' wee's gonna have a good time of it crossin'. Ah say that water looks invitin' to me. Ah feels like a pile of dust and sweat," Picker said.

Johnny's attention had been on the river since the dust settled and hadn't looked at Picker until now. His face, coated with dust, had turned white.

"Hah," Johnny laughed. "and you don't look much better either. The last one in the water is a slimy toad!" He bolted towards the river with Picker and the gelding close behind. Mathias, mules, wagon, and all, splashed into the water behind them. Once in the water the mules stopped to drink. Mathias jumped from the wagon bench and splashed about in the water, laughing and back floating. Johnny and Picker rolled off their mounts and joined him. Pickers first thought was to gain footing on the bottom, strip and begin to remove mud and grime from his body.

Johnny swam underwater and came up under Mathias and pinched him on the buttocks.

"Ouch," Mathias shouted. He turned as Johnny came up for air. "I thought a crawfish had me by the cheek, you dern fool."

Johnny laughed and swam away. "Come on, Picker," Johnny called. "I'll show you how to swim and tread water. Best you know how to stay afloat. By the look of that map we have many rivers to cross twix here and California."

They were in the water for the better part of an hour before crossing.

The river wasn't swift so the crossing was uneventful except for a hole the wagon had fallen into. The mules, however, were able to pull the wagon free.

They left the sight and sound of the gently flowing river behind them and continued their journey across the plain, refreshed after the cool bathing and swimming.

★ ★ ★ ★ ★

The sun was a couple of hours from setting when they came upon a steep grade in the trail. Mathias halted the mules at the crest. He stood up in the wagon well and peered over the hill.

Johnny surveyed the hill with concern. "Those wagoneers must of had a time of it gettin' all those big wagons down this hill," he said.

Mathias said, "They would take one wagon at a time and all the men would grasp a wheel spoke and let it down easy."

"Well, that ain't gonna work with us, Mathias. You're gonna have to hold those mules back and brake. Me and Picker ain't gonna be able to hold that wagon back all the way down. You got any rope in that wagon?"

"Nope, what you think I got here a general mercantile?" Mathias complained.

"You been able to pull everything else outta that wagon I don't see where rope is such an unusual commodity on a wagon train," Johnny argued.

"Oh well now," Mathias retorted, "I'm dern sorry to disappoint the captin."

Johnny felt his anger rising. To Picker he said, "I say we leave this cantankerous insubordinate to find his own way."

"Wow," Mathias mouthed the words 'cantankerous insubordinate', "What big words from such a small mind."

"That did it," Johnny came off his horse and ran toward the wagon. "I'm gonna turn you over my knee and thrash you."

Mathias disappeared over the far side of the wagon and the mules lurched forward to the edge of the hill. Johnny grabbed hold of one of the mule's halters. He hung on, digging in his heels. The mules stopped short before the momentum of the wagon forced them down the hill. Johnny's mare, however, saw no problem and hightailed it down the hill.

Picker, in the meantime, was standing back enjoying the exchange. "Mah. mah," he said, "but you two can sure rile yo'selves to a frenzy. I say we use dem canvas loops between dah wheels to keep dem from turnin' an' let dah wagon slide down dah hill."

"I was gonna suggest that," Mathias said with a chuckle from the other side of the wagon.

"You were gonna suggest no such a thing, " Johnny said, pointing at him. "One of these days you're gonna catch it, boy"

Mathias put his nose between his thumb and forefinger and moved up and down bending at the knees, teasing Johnny. Picker laugh heartily.

"Come on, Picker," Johnny said. "Let's get those loops off. Mathias get back up on that bench and get ready with the reins."

"Yes captin," Mathias saluted.

Picker put his hand on Johnny's shoulder. "He just teasing you, Johnny."

"I know, but sometime I forget that," Johnny said.

"You a strong boy, Johnny. Best doin forget dat," Picker advised.

"Heck, I was just gonna spank him is all."

Johnny studied the wagon, the loops, and wheels. He said, "I think one of those loops through the rear wheel spokes is all we need. The front wheels should be free for steering and braking."

"You want me to ride it down, Johnny?" Picker asked. "Mathias may lose it and get hisself hurt."

"I need your weight on the tailgate with me, Picker. We're going to hang on that tailgate to make the rear wheels dig in, that should keep the wagon from sliding and panicking the mules. If the wheels dig in too much, one of us can let go and walk behind. Mathias doesn't weigh enough to make a difference up front."

"Ah hopes we can go down slow, Picker worried. "If dat wagon gits away from us . . . " His voice trailed off as he looked down the narrow, but steep wagon path that made a slight left turn at the bottom then disappeared into some trees.

"Yeah, I know, Picker. I think it will ride down slow enough with us on the back," Johnny assured him.

"You ready up there, Mathias?" Johnny shouted.

"You sure this is gonna work, Farrell?" Mathias hollered back.

"Yep, just keep the mules straight in line. If they turn too sharp, the wagon may tip over."

"Ooooh! Then what?" Mathias questioned.

"Then you spend the rest of your life pickin' splinters out of yer behind."

"Very funny!" Mathias called back.

Johnny and Picker laughed. The plan was a good one, but Mathias had not been in on all the details. While Johnny and Picker laughed Mathias slapped the reins across the mules behinds and shouted, "Eeeyaw." The mules lurched forward over the crest of the hill followed by Picker's gelding.

Johnny shouted, "No! Wait!" He and Picker made a leap for the tail gate but missed it, falling into the dust. Peering over the hill they saw the makings of a disaster.

The mules and sliding wagon created a cloud of dust that obscured the wagons momentumous progress down the hill. Over the rumble of the wagon, fading away, came Mathias's scream, "AHHHhhhaaaawwww!"

Chapter Fourteen

DECISION AT FORT LARAMIE

After the noise of the rumbling wagon and Mathias' shouts of terror subsided, Johnny and Picker lay in the dirt atop the hill, searching the dust for signs of movement.

The dust drifted off to reveal the wagon still upright. The mules, still hitched, grazed on what appeared to be green grass. Mathias, standing up on the bench, waved and hollered.

Relieved at first to see Mathias in good health, when Johnny saw him waving from the bench he said, "Oh, oh, he must be mad as a hatter."

"Yup," Picker agreed, "Ah wouldn't be in any hurry to go down dere Ah was you."

"Reckon he'll shoot me with that derringer he's got?"

"Might," Picker smiled. "Best you let me go on down dere first and cool him down."

Picker picked himself up and walked, ran and slid down the hill. When he got to the bottom Johnny watched as Picker talked to Mathias. Then he saw Picker turn and wave to him.

Johnny hastened down the hill. When he reached the bottom, he walked into *Eden*. A clear, gentle stream flowed beneath green foliage and swirled around moss rocks. The green, fresh grass reached above their fetlocks as the horses grazed contentedly. Trees swayed gently in a cool breeze.

"Ain't this place beautiful, Johnny?" Mathias asked. "Let's camp here for a few days."

"Sure 'nuff is, Mathias. Sure is nice to see trees again."

Johnny looked the place over. "We'll let the animals graze for a day or two. Put some weight on 'em. The first time they haven't had to eat buffalo grass in quite a spell." He pulled his map from his shirt and studied it. "This must be Ash Hollow. The map has some squiggly lines here, must be that hill we just came down." Looking at Mathias out the corner of his eye, he said, "You didn't get hurt, Mathias?"

"Nope," Mathias answered. "Did you expect I would?"

"Well, no, but I heard a lot of screamin' . . ."

Picker broke in, "Ah say we set up camp and get some vittles cookin'. Ah is hungry. Let's git a fire goin'."

Looking suspiciously at Johnny, then at Picker and back to Johnny, Mathias said, "Yeah, I'm hungry too."

The fire snapped and crackled and sent a few glowing ashes into the night air. Johnny and Picker sat cross-legged near the fire, looking into the flames, conjuring images, while Mathias lay with his head propped in his left hand. They had just finished eating their supper, such as it was.

Johnny and Picker were sipping cups of coffee confiscated from Mathias' dwindling supplies. Each in his own world of thoughts, no conversation transpired between them.

The camp sight seemed to instill a peaceful ambiance that transcended the need for talk. Johnny welcomed the chance for reflection, to consider how far he had come and the things he had experienced since leaving Cornplanter on the Allegheny. The face of Joseph Schill came into focus in his mind's eye. A smile brightened his face. It gave him reason to think of Mathias, which brought him back to the present and the problem he knew he would have to confront sooner or later, the welfare of Mathias.

Johnny removed the map from inside his shirt. In the light of the fire, he pointed at *Ash Hollow*. moving his finger to the left he let it stop at *Fort Laramie.*

For some time now Johnny had been studying the idea of leaving Mathias with the troops at Fort Laramie until a wagon train arrived heading east. He could then be taken back to stay with relatives, that is, if Mathias had relatives. It occurred to him how little he knew about Mathias. Johnny hadn't discussed his idea with Mathias yet. He wasn't sure how to approach him about it without starting him on another tirade, or worse yet, giving him reason to run off on his own. Best, he thought, to wait until they arrived at Ft. Laramie. Then, if Mathias decided to make a fuss, he would be the military's responsibility. Johnny guessed, by the distance indicated on the map and the miles they had been traveling each day, they should be at Ft. Laramie in five or six days barring any unforeseen troubles.

Mathias broke the reverie of silence, "Sure is a pleasure to be layin' by a fire of burnin' wood for a change. Smellin' that wood and hearin' those snaps and crackles, watchin' those sparks risin' . . ."

"Yup," Picker agreed, "sho' ain't no pleasure sittin' by a fire burnin' dried buffalo chips."

Johnny agreed, though he remembered those buffalo chips keeping them warm on a few cold nights.

"Mathias," he said, "you got any friends back in Illinois?" He knew before he finished the question, he had said it the wrong way.

Mathias, offended, said, "Sure I got friends. You think I don't have friends?"

"I mean family, aunts or uncles?" Johnny clarified.

"I sure do. I come from a family of well to do folk, friends of the governor and folks in high places."

"Was your pa well-to-do?" Johnny asked.

"Yeah, he owned land. Sold it to purchase land in Oregon."

Johnny tried to imagine the man he buried on the trail as being well-to-do. He looked down and out last I saw him, he thought. 'course I don't know for sure what well-to-do looks like either. He thought of the Schills.

They owned land, where they well-to-do? Didn't seem like it to him, though, they were hard working and lived well for their efforts.

Pleased with the answers, Johnny finalized his plan to leave Mathias at Ft. Laramie to be returned to his people in Illinois. Relieved to know this problem was solved, he tossed a few more pieces of kindling on the fire, causing sparks to take to the air above them. Looking across the fire at Mathias, he thought, he ain't such a bad sort. His mouth is his own worse enemy, but I shall miss him. He tucked his arm under his head to prepare himself for sleep, which wasn't long in coming.

* * * * *

The trio camped two days at Ash Hollow, letting the animals renew their strength with the rest and green grass, before continuing their journey on the trail. The wheels of the mule drawn wagon turned slow, placing monotonous miles behind them. The hours became days. Johnny pulled his map from his shirt to identify an unusual rock formation rising out of the prairie. A monolith seemingly out of place in the other wise featureless prairie. They stopped and gazed across the land at *Courthouse Rock.*

"Now how do you s'pose that got there?" Mathias asked.

"The Lord put it there," Johnny answered.

"What?" Mathias said, "You mean the Lord just decided one day to up and put a rock in the middle of nowhere. For what reason?"

"So you would ask. It's those works of the Lord that remind us to humble ourselves before Him."

Johnny waited for the next remark from Mathias but it didn't come. Mathias sat on the wagon seat and gazed at the formation.

Several miles and many hours later they were rewarded with yet another and more impressive work of nature, *Chimney Rock.*

"Ah swear, Johnny," Picker said, "Ah'm humbled at dat work of dah Lawd."

"Yep," Johnny agreed, "I'm awed every day at somethin' or other. Some things He just outdone Hisself on." Studying the map he said, "It's called Chimney Rock." Looking up from his map at the rock formation, he said, "Easy to see why."

Aware they were drawing closer to Fort Laramie Johnny beckoned Picker, with a tilt of his head, to ride with him a short way ahead of Mathias and the wagon. Johnny then explained his plan to leave Mathias with the military at Fort Laramie.

"Mathias, he ain't gonna like it, Johnny," Picker said, pointing his thumb behind him. "He gonna give you a bad time."

"I know, that's why I ain't going to tell him till we get to Fort Laramie."

"Why he can't come wit us, Johnny? He no trouble. We need him an' dat wagon."

"How do you think we would have fared with the mate and constable had he been with us at Independence? Could we have moved as fast had he been with us then? He's young, Picker. He needs his folks to finish raisin' him proper. He says he's twelve. Why I bet, he isn't much past ten years. It's upon us to see he gets back to his folks. Way I see it, we saved him from certain death out there on that prairie all by hisself but where we're goin', Picker, we could very well take him to harm. I been studyin' this map." Johnny leaned towards Picker and pointed at the map. "You see these arrow like symbols and this writin' here? Well, these symbols are mountain tops, and when you have them bunched in a row like this that means a mountain range. The Rocky Mountains I'm guessin'. This writin' says 'Lakota Sioux unfriendly'. I don't know 'bout the Indians, but I think we could have trouble takin' that wagon over those mountains."

Picker studied the map and considered what Johnny pointed out. "We could leave dah wagon at Fort Laramie and Mathias could ride a mule."

"Mules are undisciplined animals for the most part, Picker, as Mathias is an undisciplined boy. The combination strikes me as dangerous."

Johnny looked toward the west and paused. "I do believe we are moving toward hard times, Picker, and I don't want to be worryin' and frettin' over Mathias all the whilst him back talkin' me so."

"You right, Johnny. You always right."

"So then, we are agreed?   We leave him at Fort Laramie?"

"Yes, Johnny," Picker said solemnly, his head bowed.

"Try to look unawares, I don't want Mathias thinkin' somethin's amiss."

Picker nodded his head and heeled his gelding riding out ahead of Johnny. Johnny understood, for he had noticed lately that Picker preferred to be alone with his grief. Maybe a part of growin' up, Johnny thought. He himself felt somehow older, or more experienced. He wasn't sure of the words to put it in place in his mind. He was sure of one thing though, cuttin' Mathias loose at Fort Laramie wasn't going to be easy.

*****

Two days later they passed Scotts Bluff and a day beyond that they approached the Laramie River. Johnny sat his mare, looking across the narrow but swift river toward the garrison at Fort Laramie. Picker reined up beside him. Mathias was still a distance behind with the wagon.

"There it is, Picker!" Johnny exhaled with a sigh. "Fort Laramie."

"Ah ain't fond of the military, Johnny," Picker said. "Ah's 'fraid dey might just try to make a soljur outta me."

"They can't do that without your permission," Johnny assured him.

"Dem folk down south made me a slave wid out my permission. If you doin mind Ah'll jest wait right here whilst you parley wid dat general in dere."

"Truth be told, Picker, I don't trust authority now either, what with the law lookin' for us and all. What you s'pose they would do if they know we're runnin' from the law."

"Dey gots two choices as Ah sees it," Picker said. "Dey hang you or make a soljur outta you. Ah's not happy to be a part of either one."

"Yeah, me either," Johnny agreed. "Let's get Mathias and that wagon across this river then we will send him on into the garrison by hisself. You and me can be on our way."

The river was only four or five feet deep. A deceptive looking river, it made up for its lack of depth by its swiftness which almost pulled Mathias, mules, wagon and all, under more than once before they reached the other side.

"Mathias!" Johnny called, riding up to the wagon that sat dripping water from every crack and crevice. He lay the rifle gently in the bed.

"Yes, Captin," Mathias answered, looking puzzled at the Hawkens.

Johnny pointed toward the garrison. "That's Fort Laramie. We're going to leave you there under the authority of the military. Me and Picker have seen you safely this far, they will see you get safely back to civilization."

Mathias looked with surprised shock at Johnny. He looked toward the garrison as if bringing himself to bare reality. He then looked at Picker with a look that said, you sold me out.

Picker lowered his head, averting his eyes from Mathias.

"Well, mebbe I don't want to go back to civilization. Mebbe I like it out here," Mathias demanded.

"You're too young, Mathias. You still need a guardian. We ain't gonna parley on this, Mathias. My minds made up."

"So," Mathias shot back, "you're gettin' rid of me, huh. Well, I don't need the likes of you two either. You've been a cactus burr in my boot all along." Mathias slapped the reins across the rumps of the mules who, reluctant as usual, moved slowly toward the garrison. "You hear me!" he shouted. "I don't need you either!"

Turning his mare toward the continuing trail, Johnny said solemnly, "Come on, Picker, we've got ground to cover before dark."

Picker, his head still lowered, reined his gelding around toward the trail.

It wasn't but a few minutes when they heard Mathias shout, "Johnny!"

Johnny and Picker turned on their mounts. Mathias had left the mule drawn wagon and ran toward them hat in hand. When he drew closer, Johnny could see he was crying. Tears were streaming down his face, dripping off his quivering chin.

Johnny wheeled his horse around. "Mathias?"

In anguish and trying to hold his tears back, Mathias twisted his hat in his hand. "Please d-don't leave me here." Mathias broke into sobs, his body convulsing in fear and grief. "Y-You're the only f-family I have, y-you and Picker."

Johnny looked over at Picker whose eyes were misting over. Mathias sniffled and struggled with more words. "I g-got no family back east, nobody. My pa was dirt poor. H-He lost the farm, couldn't sell his crops. He come to Oregon to start a new life f-for Ma and me. I-I m-miss them so." Mathias fell to his knees.

Johnny slid off his mare, knelt beside Mathias and put his arm around him. He knew that Mathias was finally releasing his pent up grief over the loss of his folks. Something Johnny himself had done in the privacy of a wooded glen he would visit in troubled times, on a hillside overlooking his beloved Allegheny River at Cornplanter.

Picker stood by his gelding with his back to the two of them, his head lowered. Johnny knew how miserable

Picker felt, not only for Mathias but in remembering his own folks and his longing to see them again.

"We won't leave you here, Mathias," Johnny said. As he stood up, he firmly gripped Mathias' shoulder.

Mathias looked up at him, sniffling and wiping tears away with his sleeve. "Thanks, Johnny. I won't give you no trouble, honest."

"Sure, I know," Johnny said. He glanced back toward the wagon. "Well, looks like your mules don't mind stayin' they're headed for the garrison. Must be the smell of the hay and oats in there. I'll go fetch them. Take my mare, Mathias, I'll catch up."

While at the garrison Johnny wrote a letter.

Joseph Schill
Volgelbacher Settlement
Clarion County, Pennsylvania

Dear Joseph,

Since I last wrote you, me and Picker picked up a friend along the trail. His name is Mathias Tibbs.

He is about your age. His folks passed on of the cholera. I am in great concern for the safety of this lad as we are entering Indian territory and I, not being too well schooled in the care and nurturing of the young, had decided to leave him at Fort Laramie to be returned to his kinfolk in the States.

I have since learned he has no kinfolk and he has expressed a strong desire to travel with me and Picker to which I have consented. I fear I have made a grievous mistake, but I anguish for him and the loss of his folks.

Your friend,
Johnny Farrell
August 1852

Johnny posted the letter at the garrison. He climbed onto the wagon bench and reined the mules toward the setting sun. It was as if someone had suddenly placed an enormous burden upon him. He was no longer responsible just for himself, but for two other human beings. A boy almost as helpless as a child and a runaway slave, just a boy himself. The three of us, Johnny thought, in a world in which every waking day is a new experience and one fraught with dangers.

Chapter Fifteen

THE STAND-OFF

Few words passed between Johnny and Picker as they rode side by side into the setting sun, the slow moving North Platte River never far from their sight. Picker was first to express his feelings on the subject of Mathias since leaving Fort Laramie.

"Mah, Ah believe Ah'd rather be kicked bloody by one of dose mules den hurt on de inside like Ah did seein' Mathias sad like dat."

"You feel the sorrow of others don't you Picker?" Johnny asked.

"Dey make me think of mah own sorrows, Johnny, but sometime dah sorrow of others make mah sorrows seem less somehow. Ain't no explainin' it."

"Yeah. Know what you mean."

They fell into silence again, the miles moving along under the hooves of the horses and mules. Johnny reflected on his decision to take Mathias along. He was still troubled about it. He had talked to one of the soldiers at the fort when he went to retrieve the mules. What the soldier had told him kept repeating in his mind, "Son, yer over a month late gettin' here and yer not even half way to Californy and the worse part of the journey is ahead of you. I were you I'd hook up with one of the trains headed back to the states."

"Can't go back," he had told him. "Got to go on."

"What's troublin' you, Johnny?" Picker asked, bringing Johnny out of his thoughts.

"What makes you think somethin's troublin' me?" Johnny asked him.

"You awfully quiet an' trouble is showin' on your face."

"I was just thinkin' 'bout Mathias," Johnny said. "I tried to do what was right for him, Picker."

"Ah know dat, an' Ah think Mathias know dat too."

"We have already run into danger and near death," Johnny went on, "and we ain't half way to California and I'm told that was the easy part."

Johnny picked his words thoughtfully not wanting to upset Picker but at the same time wanting him to know the truth as he saw it. "You ever hear of the Donner train, Picker?"

"No," Picker answered with a hesitation in his voice as if he wasn't sure he wanted to hear.

"They got caught in a winter snow storm in the Sierra Mountains of California 'cause they were late gettin' there. Most of them froze to death and worse."

Picker looked at Johnny sideways. "Are we late, Johnny?" he asked.

"Yep, we're late," Johnny answered.

They traveled on in silence a few more miles or so before Johnny pointed out another troublesome sign.

"Look it there now. See those graves? We been passin' graves and abandoned wagons all along this trail. This is a trail of death, Picker! Now we're in Lakota territory. I sure hope they don't mind our trespass."

Picker took a vigilant look around them.

Picker, Johnny thought, could handle himself if trouble came. Mathias, on the other hand, was a quick tempered boy with a gun. Another worry Johnny had been nurturing.

"I sure didn't expect all this worryin' when I launched my raft into the Allegheny last spring. I didn't expect I would be nursemaidin' a boy in the wilderness. Just takin' care of myself seemed proper enough task to me."

"Mah Mammy has tol' me dah Lawd works in mysterious ways, Johnny," Picker said.

"Yup," Johnny agreed, "and when I look at all those graves I am impressed with just how mysterious are His ways."

Johnny took the map out again and scanned its surface.

"It's gettin dark, Picker. Map says there is a place called Warm Springs up ahead. Sounds like a good place to bathe. Seems when I bathe in that Platte River I get more mud on me than I'm takin' off."

"Sho' nuff," Picker agreed.

Johnny turned on his mount to beckon Mathias on. "Come on, Mathias, swimmin' hole up ahead," he said, pointing up the trail.

* * * * *

The days wore long and hot into weeks as they traveled deeper into Indian country. Johnny and Picker rode side by side for miles and sometimes days without uttering a word. The heat sapped too much strength and even talking seemed an unnecessary waste of energy. Dozing off, while riding along on their mounts, became a common occurrence. Sometimes the horses wandered off the trail. At those times Mathias enjoyed the inclination to shout at Johnny, ordering him back on the trail.

"Hey, Farrell, git your butt back on the trail. Where in tarnation you think your goin', to Canada or somethin'? Geez, it's a good thing you got somebody 'round here can follow a trail." At this Picker would snicker and Johnny would feel his anger rising while looking heavenward; then all fell back into the routine of travel along the trail.

Again Johnny's eye lids drooped as his mare rocked him gently through the shimmering heat of the desert-like prairie floor; silent except for a faint squeak of the wheels or the tinkling of harness rings from Mathias' wagon, or the raking call of a locust beckoning through the heat of day. Other life, both predator and prey, slept in the cool of their burrows or what shade could be found, waiting out the heat until the cool of the evening.

On the edge of drifting into a dream, Johnny was awakened abruptly by a blood curdling scream and the thunder of many hooves a short distant to his front. He halted his mare and focused his eyes on a startling sight.

From a rise to his right a dozen or so horsemen, he recognized immediately as Indians and assumed were Sioux, rode down on a herd of buffalo.

The prairie was suddenly alive with activity as the buffalo herd started into a run, turning north. The Indians, riding up beside them, shot arrows deep into thick hides. They rode with legs wrapped around their ponies as if man and beast were one.

"We dang near walked right into the middle of that herd!" Mathias shouted as he pulled the wagon up next to Picker and Johnny. "What's with you two anyhow? You can't even see a herd of grazin' buffalo?"

"Stow it, Mathias," Johnny ordered, raising his arm to beckon silence. "I'd guess those Indians are more interested in them buffalo than us. Let's just keep on movin' like we was."

Wide awake now they ambled along the trail, watching the skill of the Indians with great interest. The Indians rode their ponies among the herd, shooting arrows deep into hide and muscle.

"Them folks have their work to do now," Johnny observed. "Must be a dozen or so buffalo lyin' on the ground there for butcherin'. What a sight to see the way they come off that hill into the middle of that herd, shootin' as they rode. Amazin', absolutely amazin'."

"Coulda been us they come ridin' down on," Mathias complained. "You two must be fallin' to sleep up there."

"Well, if they decide to come ridin' down on us like that, not much we can do about it anyhow, Mathias," Johnny assured him.

"If you can't stay awake, drive this wagon a spell. Anybody could fall asleep on this wagon could fall asleep on a battlefield."

"Yeah, I'll drive that wagon a spell, Mathias," Johnny said. "Anything to keep you happy. You can ride my mare."

Truth be told, I was not on guard, Johnny thought as he dismounted. Mathias was right. I fell asleep and could have gotten us all killed.

Johnny pulled himself onto the wagon bench and took up the reins. For assurance, Johnny touched the stock of the Hawkens rifle, that lay across his thighs. He edged the wagon slowly past the scene of half nude squaws, kneeling by the carcasses of the buffalo. With quick motions their knives deftly sliced open the bellies of the great animals and skinned back the hides. By now blood covered most of their bodies.

Leading Picker and Mathias by a short distance, Johnny drove the wagon close by one of the buffalo carcasses that lay near the trail. A squaw looked up and smiled. Johnny smiled back. Just then the woman withdrew a bloody hand from inside the cavity and raised a hand full of bloody goo as if offering it to Johnny. Johnny had butchered many deer and recognized the bloody goo as the liver. The woman brought the liver up to her mouth and took a healthy bite of it. As the blood dripped from her mouth onto her bosom her eyes rolled as if she had just tasted of the victuals of a French cuisine. Indeed, Johnny thought, to her it was.

Johnny smiled, brought his hand to the brim of his hat and urged the mules forward with a slap of the reins. His stomach did a hunger growl as he imagined that liver roasting on a spit over a campfire. I wonder if it tastes as good a deer liver? he asked himself.

The braves, who were now whooping and waving their bows apparently in celebration of a successful hunt, circled back toward the fallen bison. One looked toward the wagon. Leaving the others behind he advanced on his pony, bringing it to a canter as he came near.

Johnny tapped the Hawkens again and felt his heart begin to pound a little harder as a shot of fear rose within him. He placed two load wads in his mouth, then fingered the lead balls in the pouch and caps in his pocket as he kept the wagon moving.

The Indian noticed the rifle, slowed his pony to a walk and came on slowly to Johnny's right. Johnny knew immediately what that meant. He was at a disadvantage. Johnny, being right-handed, always fired with the butt of the weapon against his right shoulder. The weapon lay across his lap with the barrel pointing to his left which meant he would have to swing it around if it was needed, wasting precious seconds.

Johnny was awed by the size of the bronze man sitting tall on his blanket saddle. He must be all of six feet, or at least seemed that way, he thought. Not handsome, but austere with coal black hair that hung in braids over his shoulders and lay across his naked chest.

"What're we gonna do, Johnny?" Mathias whispered nervously behind him.

In a normal but firm voice Johnny said, "Just keep walking that mare forward, Mathias. Show no fear."

Picker rode to Johnny's left. Johnny shot him a glance and saw no fear in his manner.

The big Indian brought his pony alongside the wagon and peered in as if looking for something. He still held his bow but Johnny could see his quiver was empty, all his arrows having been expended in the hunt. A knife hung from a crude scabbard at his side. He stopped suddenly and stared at Picker with a look of mild shock. He came back to Johnny, indicated the rifle across Johnny's lap and said. "Trade buffalo meat for rifle."

Johnny now realized why the Indian looked into the wagon. He saw that they had no supplies. This Indian is no dummy, he thought. He brought the mules to a halt.

"No," Johnny answered. "No trade rifle."

"Hah," the Indian scoffed, "I take rifle."

Johnny tensed at the threat, but before he could react Mathias said from behind him.

"You want me to shoot him, Johnny?"

Johnny turned to see Mathias had eased the mare up next to the wagon and had the derringer pointed at the Indian's head.

The Indian looked with surprise at Mathias and was visibly curious of the small object in Mathias' hand. He leaned forward on his mount and stared intently at the derringer. Then he sat back on his mount and turned toward the rest of the hunting party who were watching the exchange. He regained his proud and arrogant perch.

The seconds seemed like hours to Johnny. The minute Mathias pulled out that derringer and aimed it at the Indian the scene had changed. The Indian had been challenged and could not back down with his braves looking on. Johnny knew Indians well enough to know their pride would not let them see reason. Death was preferred to cowardice in the eyes of his tribe.

"Put the gun away, Mathias," Johnny demanded.

"He ain't gettin' that rifle, Johnny," Mathias said, still pointing the derringer at the Indian's head.

"Mathias, is this rifle worth your life?" Johnny asked.

"This Indian is gonna die first, Johnny. Unless he backs off."

"He ain't gonna back off, Mathias. He can't."

"What do you mean, he can't? If he's got a brain in his head at all, he'll turn 'round and walk," Mathias said, looking straight into the Indian's eyes.

"It ain't got nothin' to do with brains, Mathias. Now put that gun away."

"No sir, I got the upper hand here and I say he walks. You hear that Indian? Turn 'round and walk," Mathias ordered. "You ain't takin' nothin'."

Johnny knew it would do no more good to reason with Mathias then it would with the Indian. This was a clash of cultures. Neither one understanding the other.

Beads of perspiration began to form over Johnny's brow. He knew two Indians would die here today. One from Mathias' derringer and one from the rifle, but he also knew he, Mathias and Picker would die very soon afterward.

Suddenly a scream came from the direction of the busy women. Johnny looked to his front in time to see a huge monster, standing on its hind legs on a ridge to his left. The monster was not but fifty yards from the blood-covered woman when it roared, went down on all fours and began to run down the slope, crazed by the smell of the buffalo carrion. The blood splashed woman was as fair a prey to the grizzly as was the buffalo.

The big Indian reached toward his empty quiver and with a look of shock and disappointment drew his knife instead. He reined his unwilling pony around hard and rode off toward the bear.

Johnny gave no thought at all to his next move. It came natural as his instincts beckoned him to survival. In one swift but smooth movement, he raised the rifle to his shoulder, aimed and fired. In a matter of seconds he re-loaded--powder, wad, ball 'n cap--and fired again.

Chapter Sixteen

A BEAR DIES AND BUZZARDS FLY

Mouth agape, Picker sat his mount.

Mathias, sitting upon the mare, holding his derringer at arm's length, aimed at nothing.

Johnny stood in the bench well of the wagon and calmly reloaded the rifle. He sat down and placed the rifle upright before him. As he began to think about what he had done he had to conceal, as best he could, the shaking in his hands as waves of tension settled over him.

The barrel of the rifle was still warm as he had fired three times at the grizzly before it finally collapsed at the feet of the frightened woman. The first lead ball stopped the bears run. It raised itself on its hind legs and turned toward Johnny, swinging its great head in ferocious contempt.

As if performing a strange ballet, using left and right hand in harmonious fashion, Johnny maneuvered rifle, powder, wad, ball, rod and cap; raised and fired. The giant grizzly swayed in his towering posture. Stunned it went down on all fours, snorting a mist of blood from its nose, staring with glazed but searing eyes at Johnny. Just as it began to advance toward him Johnny fired once more. The bear pulled its great head in, falling in a heap on its side. The woman stumbled backward falling upon the bull she had been cutting.

The big Indian had stopped his pony abruptly after the first report and watched with amazement as Johnny reloaded, fired and reloaded, his eyes moving from Johnny to grizzly after each blast.

The rest of the hunting party, scrambling to recover arrows, barely had time to set arrow to bow before it was all over.

"Picker!" Johnny beckoned with the big Indian out of earshot.

Coming out of mild shock Picker answered, "Yessah!'"

"Johnny," Johnny said under his breath. "I'm Johnny. Remember?"

"Yeah, ahh, Yeah. Ah hears yah."

Johnny removed his knife from its scabbard and handed it to Picker. "I have three lead balls in that bear I want back," he said. "You think you can dig 'em out? There should be two in his lungs and one in the skull between the eyes. Gonna take some effort to get the one in his skull. Wouldn't mind havin' a cut or three of bear meat for supper if you don't mind. I'll parley with our big friend there. I'm hopin' we earned some respect."

"Sho' nuff, Johnny. Dat was some shootin', Johnny. Some shootin'," Picker said as he rode away toward the fallen bear.

The Indians sat their mounts as Picker went about the task of retrieving the lead.

The big Indian walked his pony back to the wagon. Johnny collected himself and looked to Mathias who had lowered his arm. Staring at the bear, he still held the derringer.

"Put that gun away, Mathias. We won't be needin' it, I don't think."

"Oh, ah yeah," Mathias said, putting the derringer back inside his vest. "Don't think I've ever seen that rifle fired like that before. Don't even think my grandpa could do that. You justify havin' it, Johnny."

"I had a good teacher, Mathias," Johnny answered. He thought of his pa and the hunting they used to do in the hills of Pennsylvania. He had to admit though, he had never seen a bear as big as that grizzly. Pennsylvania black bear don't get nearly that size, he thought. He wished his pa had seen how well he had done. Then he remembered who had taught his pa how to handle a rifle so well, John Vogelbacker himself. The expert woodsman and hunter of the Black Forest of Germany, the man who shot nine deer with one lead ball. "Yup, I had a good teacher," Johnny repeated.

"Mathias, did you figger out how that fellow shot nine deer with one lead ball?"

"No," Mathias said. "I lost most of a nights sleep tryin' and come to the conclusion you was joshin'."

Johnny's head came up in laughter as the Indian approached.

"No, wasn't joshin'. Go help Picker with that bear," Johnny said, wanting to get Mathias as far away from the Indian as possible.

The Indian approached the wagon with his right hand raised. Johnny hoped that meant the same to these Indians as it did to the Indians of Pennsylvania, the sign of friendship. He raised his own right hand in hopes that it did.

"What your name?" the Indian asked with a strong voice.

"Johnny Farrell from Corn . . ." Johnny stopped realizing it would be useless to continue. "Johnny," he said.

"Jon-nay, Jon-nay," the Indian said in halted English. "You save life of woman. I have not seen such a thing as this. Never have I seen the 'bear that walks like a man' die so quickly. You have great power with rifle. Some day you teach me?"

"Someday, yes, but today I don't have enough lead to teach you," Johnny explained.

"What is this 'lead'?" the Indian asked.

Johnny took out the pouch of lead ball he had tied to his belt and gave one to the Indian.

"Oooohh," the Indian responded and then placed the ball between his teeth and bit down. "Aaaahh," he said, his eyes brightening. "I bring you lead, you teach me."

"You know where this lead?" Johnny asked.

"I bring you lead, you teach me," the Indian repeated.

"Yes." Johnny felt safe in answering, feeling quite sure he would never be seeing this Indian again anyhow.

"Now," the Indian continued. "I give you gift for what you have done." He turned and shouted a command to the other hunters sitting their ponies nearby. "You have no food in your wagon."

"No, we have no food. We kill rabbits and antelope along the trail and eat them. We have no salt to cure what we don't eat."

"We give you salt and buffalo meat. We give you three buffalo hides, you make robes for winter. You maybe give us bear?"

"Yes," Johnny said. His hand sweeping toward the hunters bringing up the hides, buffalo meat, and salt wrapped in the buffalo hide. "We are grateful for these gifts of meat, salt and hides for we must travel far. You take bear, we take lead from bear." Johnny stood up in the wagon and hollered toward Picker. "Picker. Just dig out the lead and leave the bear for the Indians!"

Picker waved in acknowledgment.

At that moment the woman whose life Johnny had saved, now wearing a buckskin dress, walked up to the wagon holding something attached to a rawhide cord. She spoke to the big Indian in their tongue. The big Indian looked at her with mild shock and exchanged words with her. Johnny thought it sounded like he was arguing with her, or trying to dissuade her.

The big Indian turned to Johnny and said, "Woman wants you to have gift. This gift means much to her. It is her Dreamcatcher."

Johnny was stunned. He had heard of the Dreamcatcher but had never seen one. He knew of its importance to the owner. He looked at the big Indian with concern, but knew to refuse a gift offered was an insult to an Indian. He stepped down from the wagon bench, walked to the woman and knelt down on one knee. The woman raised the loop above his head and lowered it around Johnny's neck.

Johnny took the Dreamcatcher in his hand. It was a looped stick with webbing in the center that fit in the palms of his hands. It had three feathered tassels hanging from the bottom. In the center of the loop and webbing was an open circle. Johnny understood that the webbing was to catch all the bad dreams. Only good dreams passed through the open circle in the center.

Johnny's eyes burned with tears as he looked up at the woman and said, "Thank you, I shall wear it proudly. If I should give it as a gift, as you have, it shall be with the same goodness in my heart."

The big Indian told the woman what Johnny had said. They exchanged words, then the woman turned with a smile and walked away.

The Indian turned to Johnny and said, "She say, 'your eyes say you have goodness in your heart.'"

Johnny climbed back onto the wagon bench. The meat, salt and hides loaded up in the wagon, the Indian raised his right hand again and said, "Travel well, Jon-nay." He reined his pony around and began to ride away.

Johnny hollered after him, "What is your name?"

The Indian turned his pony around. Swinging his right arm against his chest, he said proudly, "Ta-tan-ka I-yo-ta-ke."

"Farewell, To-tan-ka I-yo-ta-ke." Johnny repeated the name over and over again to set it into his memory.

Picker and Mathias reined in beside Johnny and the wagon. "Ah gots only two lead balls, Johnny." Picker handed the flattened and twisted lead to Johnny.

"Yeah, that ball went clean through the bears head," Mathias said. "Couldn't find it nowheres. You musta packed a lot of powder in that load. Lucky you didn't breach the barrel."

"Did what I had to do, Mathias. I ain't never seen a bear that big. Anyhow we have us lot's of meat and salt for the rest of our journey thanks to To-tan-ka I-yo-ta-ke."

It had been some time since their last antelope kill. Their graving for food, especially red meat, was becoming intense.

"I can see a buffalo liver roasting on a stick and it's makin' me hungry. We'll be makin' camp soon."

"Liver!" Mathias screwed up his face. "Yuk! I'll take a good steak anytime."

"Dat makin' me hungry too." Picker agreed.

"Which?" Mathias asked. "The steak or the liver?"

"Both!" Picker answered and they all laughed.

* * * * *

Since leaving Warm Springs a month earlier they had been traveling on the hot prairie basin with rising mountains off in the distance. Johnny knew they would soon be crossing those mountains.

Their encounter with the Lakota Sioux two weeks before was ever present on Johnny's mind. They were very fortunate the way things turned out. Johnny acknowledged how differently events could have gone down, but he felt a certain amount of security in knowing he had made a friend. It is possible to deal with these plainsmen, he thought. The stories he had heard and read may not be true at all. Johnny looked at the Dreamcatcher and tucked it inside his shirt.

Johnny was deep in thought upon his mare when Picker yelled, "Look!"

Johnny reined in his mare sharply and looked toward the western sky where Picker was pointing. At a distance, high above, buzzards circled lazily over the hot plains. He watched as they funneled down toward the prairie floor. Slowly circling lower, following one another, then disappearing over the rise.

Picker drew up beside Johnny. "Looks to be like dem buzzards found demselves some vittles," he said.

"Yup, possibly a dead buffalo or two."

Mathias caught up with the wagon in time to see the buzzards descending over the horizon.

"I don't like it," he said, his face drawing a look of grief.

"Don't like what?" Johnny asked.

"The buzzards," Mathias said, "they know you're gonna die before you do. They give me the shivers."

"Yup," Johnny said, "I heard tell they know death is nearby. The smell of a rotting carcass rises with the heat, I s'pose."

"No, I mean they know *before* you die. They know you're dying. They circled Manley's wagon train before the cholera hit. They seemed to know." Mathias was soft spoken almost to a whisper.

"Oh, dat's scary," Picker said. Then with humor in his voice, he said, "Come to think on it, Ah haven't heard any wolves in dah past couple nights. All dah scavengers in dah desert must be over der havin' a picnic."

"Ain't no laughing matter what's goin' on over that rise, Picker," Mathias barked.

"You're awful grim, Mathias," Johnny said. "Buzzards are nature's way of cleaning up. They're just clearin' the prairie of a rotten mess of buffalo carcass."

They continued on their way. Johnny's curiosity beckoned him toward the rise.

"I'm not sure I want to go ridin' into a pile of rotting buffalo carcass," Mathias said. "Mebbe we can circle around. The stench'll soon be on the breeze, that'll be bad enough."

"Geez, Mathias," Johnny quipped, "you're makin' me hungry talkin' like that."

Johnny and Picker broke into an outburst of laughter. Mathias grimaced.

They were still laughing when they reached the crest of the ridge. Johnny suddenly drew hard rein. His laughter was quickly replaced by a cruel furrow across his brow.

At first stunned speechless, the sight he beheld brought him to prayer. "Oh Lord God help us," he gasped.

His mare became restive and tried to turn around and run. Johnny fought her to a compromise sideways on the ridge. From there he looked upon a scene of carnage rendered forth from the shallow valley before him.

Bloated and partially devoured remains of men, women and oxen lay about in various positions where they had fallen among charred ruins of wagons some weeks before. Wolves and coyotes argued with growls and nips over the morsels of human flesh, the vultures cleaned up their leftovers.

A half moan, half cry emanated from Mathias. "I knew it," he said.

The breeze shifted and the stench waft over the three. The horses and mules were becoming impossible to control. Picker flew off his gelding, held tight to the reins and retched: his ejection flying about as he fought his horse.

Mathias, upon witnessing Pickers reaction, disgorged as well over the side of the wagon. The mules bolted, turning to the east. The wagon traveled a distance, with Picker in pursuit, before Mathias gained control upwind of the devastation. There he and Picker waited for Johnny to catch up.

Johnny walked his mare slowly toward Picker and Mathias. All three in various states of mild shock there was no conversation for some time. Each dealing with his feelings in his own way. Mathias sat on the wagon bench, gazing down the trail toward the east, holding the reins with his elbows on his knees.

Picker stood by his gelding, holding the reins, looking away from the rise that concealed the death scene.

Johnny dismounted, then crouched down on bended knees and toes. He picked up a dried stick and made figures in the dust, trying to rid his mind of the sight he had just witnessed. He knew full well what they had to do next and believed neither Picker nor Mathias had the stomach for it. He kept tapping the stick on the ground before him.

After long moments, Mathias broke the silence. "That was the Manley train," he said thinly.

"What?" Johnny asked.

"That was the Manley train," Mathias repeated.

"Yeah, figgered as much, they was the last train leaving Independence. It could be a train from another trail out of Saint Joe, mebbe, there are only four wagons there." Johnny suggested.

"I know those wagons. I been seein' the others along the trail. Wasn't sure then, but I am now. Poor Charlie," Mathias said, this time almost inaudible.

"Charlie?" Johnny questioned.

"Yeah, Charles William Fulbright the third he called himself. I used to call him Charlie to make him angry."

"That figures," Johnny said.

"I was just joshin' him. I liked Charlie," Mathias insisted. He began to sob.

"Yeah, I remember him. Seemed like a nice boy. His mother was nice too. Mebbe his was one of the graves we past along the trail. Mebbe he died peacefully."

"No, I checked the names on all those graves. His wasn't among them," Mathias said, wiping his tears. "He sure was a know-it-all though. Always correctin' my talkin'."

Johnny suddenly thought of the girl with the curls. The one on the boat that tossed Picker the potatoes and smiled at him from the wagon seat in Independence.

Grim visions began to form in his mind. He imagined one of those grotesque forms that lay upon the ground over the ridge as being the pretty girl.

"Oh no!" he groaned. Casting a sideways look at Picker Johnny could see he must have been thinking the same thing. "Mathias, do you remember a young girl 'bout my age with long curly hair?"

"Yeah," he answered in an almost inaudible voice. "That was Becky Fergeson. Didn't see her name along the trail either. I felt happy not seein' their names on those wooden crosses and boards. I gave no thought to the poor folk who were in those graves. Your right, Johnny, I sure am a peezer."

Picker stood shaking his lowered head, "Oh Lawdy, Lawdy. Dah least Ah can do fo' her is bury her proper. Ah would've starved to death fo' sho' if not fo' her."

Johnny acknowledged the truth in Picker's words as he looked back toward the ridge. His faith shaken, he questioned. How could God let someone so good die so young and horribly?

Chapter Seventeen

THE BURIAL DETAIL

It had to be the middle of August by now, near as Johnny could figure. The midsummer heat of the prairie basin would exacerbate the gruesome task of burying the victims of the Manley wagon train. They had already decided to dig one large grave for all the remains rather than dig separate graves. The sooner this job was done the better for all. Johnny was concerned about Picker and Mathias, especially Mathias.

Johnny carried the only spade they had over his shoulder as the three of them walked slowly up the ridge, leaving the animals behind.

"What do you 'spose killed them?" Mathias asked.

"Don't know. Mebbe the cholera," Johnny answered.

"How'd dah wagons git burned?" Picker asked.

"Don't know," Johnny answered. "Mebbe they burned the bodies to purify against the disease."

"Yeah, cholera kills fast," Mathias offered. "Ma was feelin' fine in the morning, started feelin' poorly at noon and was gone by evenin'. It ain't no lingering sickness that's for sure."

"Must be what happened. They just stopped on the trail. Couldn't go no further. Each died in his turn," Johnny surmised.

"Lawdy, Lawdy," Picker groaned.

They stopped at the top of the ridge, removed their shirts and tied them around their faces to stifle the stench and guard against disease, then made their way toward the ghastly scene.

Hours later they had the single grave deep enough to accept all the bodies. Now the worst moment was upon them, gathering up bodies and body parts and bringing them to the grave site.

Johnny ventured forward to the first body, laying face down beside a wagon turned on its side. It was a man, he could tell by the clothing. The britches which housed the bloated remains were stretched to their limits. One arm was folded under the body. Johnny rolled the body over. The distorted face of Captain Manley stared up at him with cold vacant eyes. Johnny's attention was quickly drawn to the chest area where worms crawled in and out of a blackened hole. The dried and blackened stain on the white shirt inside the vest revealed a broken, multicolored stick protruding from the chest. The hand was wrapped firmly around the stick. At the end of the stick were three small rows of closely gathered feathers.

"Picker! Mathias!" he shouted. "Come here quick!"

"You find something, Johnny?" Mathias asked, approaching in no special hurry.

"This is Capt'n Manley, ain't it Mathias?"

Mathias gave the face a quick once over then looked away. "Yeah, looks like."

Johnny pulled the arrow from Captain Manley's chest. "He was killed by an arrow. Probably the last to die. Did he carry a rifle, Mathias?" Johnny asked.

"Yeah, strapped to his horse. I don't see any dead horses here come to think on it."

"Yeah, and no rifles either. The Indians took 'em. Capt'n Manley here must've held his ground by this wagon. This is the only wagon that is not burned. The Indians must have left in a hurry after the capt'n expired."

"Or before," Mathias added.

"What do you mean, Mathias?" Johnny asked.

"I looked around for Charles and Becky, they ain't here. Mebbe they took them," Mathias said.

"Who took dem?" Picker asked.

"Whoever put this arrow in Capt'n Manley's chest, Picker," Johnny answered.

"Dat mean dey still alive den," Picker said with hope in his voice.

Johnny looked around in different directions. "Yes, thank God. It looks that way. But why?" he wondered.

"Why?" Mathias asked.

"Why would they kill all the others and leave those two alive?" Johnny asked.

"They weren't the only two, Johnny. There were more children on that train." Mathias added, "and Manpreet Coonwaller too."

"Man what?" Johnny asked surprised.

"Manpreet Coonwaller," Mathias said. "He'd steal the pants right off you if you didn't keep your belt tight. Didn't like him. Nobody did. He was a mix blood, copper skinned boy 'bout your age, Johnny. His ma was from India, believe he said. His pa was a farmer from Ohio. His ma ran off when his pa decided they were comin' to California to find gold. She's probably back in India by now. Anyhow ol' Manpreet was a mean boy, and cold blooded. I saw him kill a camp dog and eat it for supper."

"Lot'sa folk eat dog, Mathias," Picker said.

"Not on a wagon train, Picker. Thing is, he enjoyed the kill. You shudda seen the look in his eyes when he did it. Gave me the shivers." Mathias eyed the area again, "I was kind of hopin' I would find his body here. If I had a choice of being alone in the wilderness with a war party of Indians or Manpreet, I think I'd rather take my chances with the war party."

"You think he could have done all this, Mathias?" Johnny asked.

"If that had been a knife stickin' outta Manley's chest I'd given it thought. Knowin' him though, he probably ran and hid when the trouble began."

"Did you tease him about his name, Mathias?" Johnny couldn't resist the question.

"No ma'am," Mathias answered. "Rather tease a rattlesnake."

"Let's get these poor folks under ground." Johnny said, "I got some cogitatin' to do 'bout all this an' I'm gettin' hot and sick wrapped up in this shirt. I can't breathe and don't want to breathe what there is to breathe."

"Oh, oh Farrell's gonna do some cogin'," Mathias teased. "Everybody watch out for the answers he's liable to come up with."

"Mathias," Picker shook his head, "dis ain't dah time for dat now."

"He started it, Picker. Anyhow, I'm just tryin' to take my mind off all this. I'm gettin' sick again too."

Before nightfall, the bodies buried and final prayers said, the three sat in Mathias' wagon upwind and a distance away from the rotting remains of the oxen.

"I don't think I'll ever get the smell outta my nose," Mathias complained.

"Yeah," Johnny agreed. Pulling the map from his shirt, he searched the trail ahead of them for the nearest river. "We got some distance to go before we reach the Sweetwater River. When we get there, I'm gonna sit in it till I feel clean again if it takes all day."

"What we gonna do 'bout dem chillin's, Johnny?" Picker asked, "Mebbe dey lost out der somewheres."

"I been cogin' on that, Picker," Johnny said, looking sideways at Mathias. "Mebbe they're lost or mebbe they're dead or mebbe they're with Indians who don't exactly fancy to given them back just 'cause we ask."

"You mean the Indians may have taken them captives?" Mathias asked.

"I've heard tell of things like that, Mathias. Anyhow I'm just spellin' out the possibilities."

"What dis 'captives'?" Picker asked.

"That's what we were on the *Mary Louise*, Picker," Johnny reminded him.

Picker sat back with a frown on his face and said nothing.

"In the mornin' we'll try to pick up their trail," Johnny continued, "but we all got to agree on this 'cause it ain't gonna be easy. You see those mountains to the west? We've got to cross them somewhere and the winter storms will start soon up there. If we spend too much time tryin' to find the young'uns we could perish ourselves. Those young'uns just might perish with us if we git them back. They might be better off with the Indians."

"Ah can't see anybody bein' better off a captive," Picker said.

"Who says they're captives," Mathias shot back. "That's just some of Farrell's cogin'."

"You don't think we should go after them, Mathias?" Johnny asked.

"Well, yeah. Like I said, I liked Charlie, but I don't see any sense in us all freezin' in those mountains when there is a chance they're better off with the Indians. 'Least 'til next spring," Mathias offered.

"Yep, you got a point, Mathias. Course by next spring we will never find them. Best to go after them now while the trail is fresh."

"What are we gonna do when we find them? One of those young'uns is a baby almost. A wailin' and cryin' baby," Mathias emphasized.

"I can't argue with you, Mathias, you make sense." Johnny agreed. "Let's sleep on it tonight and we will decide in the mornin'."

The crickets chirped in unceasing harmony. A serenade that always lulled Johnny to sleep at night, but this night was as different as the day had been. A day like none he had ever lived before.

With a troubled mind, Johnny watched the stars roll by in their perpetual journey across the heavens. Ominous imaginations clouded his reasoning when he gave thought to following the trail in search of the survivors of the wagon train. Knowing full well the dangers involved, he still asked himself, how could he not go after them?

He listened to the restive breathing of Picker and Mathias while in constant effort of trying to rid his own mind of the grotesque images of decaying bodies.

Suddenly, a scream of terror in the darkness brought him and Picker to the a sitting position. The scream came from Mathias.

"Maaa! Where are you Ma?"

"Mathias!" Johnny reached toward him. "Wake up, boy. Wake up. You're having a bad dream. Everything's fine, Mathias. It's all over. No harm will come to you. I've got the ol' Hawkens right here, no harm will come to you."

"I-I had a dream I rolled over a body and it was you, Johnny, starin' at me like ol' Captn' Manley," Mathias stammered, his body shaking. "I ran to another body and it was Picker starin' at me. Every time I looked at a body it was one of you. I was all alone out there with all them bodies. I looked for Ma, but she was nowhere around."

"Ah not dead, Mathias," Picker assured him, "Ah right here. Ah doin leave you alone."

"Johnny, I'm glad you didn't leave me at Fort Laramie. I know you was just tryin' to do right by me. You two are like family 'cause you know'd my ma and pa even if only for a little while. There's some meanin' there. You know what I mean, Johnny?"

"Yeah, I think so," Johnny admitted. "Anyhow we're stuck with each other now, the three of us."

"Yep," Mathias said, "you're stuck with me huh, Johnny."

"Yep, I'm stuck with you, Mathias."

"Hah," Mathias laughed, "Farrell's stuck with me. How 'bout that, Picker. Ain't that funny?"

"Go to sleep, you peezer!" Johnny said with half a smile on his face. He heard Picker muffling a laugh in the darkness.

Chapter Eighteen

THE SEARCH

He opened his eyes to the early hours of dawn. For Johnny, first awakening had always been a good experience. Even the weeks aboard the *Mary Louise* had not changed that. Today, however, was different. Somehow he felt years older. Like he had gone to sleep for twenty years and woke up with the mind of a tired old man, but wiser. The young don't concern themselves with death, he thought. That is the curiosity of the older folk. But now he knew the true eminence of death. The power that death eventually held over life, always waiting in the wings for it's time to appear; sometimes expected, sometimes not, but always there, waiting. Waiting especially for the foolish who would tempt it.

The looming mountains to the west shrouded in white cumulus clouds like gigantic mounds of cotton beckoned Johnny to hurry on, while a sense of moral obligation told him to track the party of unshod ponies and find the surviving members of the Manley train. These were not pleasant thoughts with which to awaken on this hot August morning somewhere deep in Indian territory.

"Hey, Farrell!" came a shout with a Mathias tone to it. "You gonna sleep all day?"

Johnny forced himself to sit up in the wagon. He looked around for Picker and Mathias. He saw Picker mounted on his gelding and over his shoulder Mathias sat on the wagon bench, whip in hand and mules hitched. They had already broken camp and were ready to roll.

"We let you sleep, Johnny," Picker said from his mount. "Figgered you needed dah rest."

"That was Picker's idea," Mathias said, "I figgered you had enough rest. You had me awake all night with your snorin'."

"Dat was only dis mornin', Mathias," Picker said.

"What about your nightmares, Mathias," Johnny insisted. "Who could sleep through that?"

"What nightmares?" Mathias retorted.

Johnny looked over at Picker who just grinned and shrugged his shoulders.

"Forget it," Johnny said, jumping out of the wagon. "I 'preciate your letting me sleep."

"Ah found dah tracks of ponies leavin' dah main trail headed north, Johnny," Picker said, "Are we goin' after dem?"

"We have no choice, Picker. Our fates have been sealed in the matter. We will have to trust in God to get us through those mountains. I have no notion at all when, or even if, we will get to California. God help us."

"Well, I don't have the abidin' faith you have, Farrell," Mathias spoke up. "I say we continue on to California."

"It's 'bout time you acquired some abidin' faith, Mathias. Like I said before, it may help your disposition some."

Picker laughed a hardy laugh and they all moved out, following the tracks in the hot prairie dust.

The three tracked the Indians northward until the trail turned west toward the mountains. They crossed unnamed rivers and valleys each day, bringing the majestic mountains closer. Soon they reached the first range and began to climb a narrowing mountainous trail. It became apparent to Johnny the wagon would have to be abandoned.

"Unhitch those mules, Mathias. We'll leave the wagon here and use it as a guide-on when we come back. Come on, Picker, let's load one of the mules with the supplies. Mathias can ride one and we can all take turns leading the other."

*****

The days soon became weeks and still the only sign of Indians were the fading pony tracks. They were no longer sure they were even the same ponies. They had crossed other trails on the way, but Picker was insistent that the trail they were on was the right one. Johnny wasn't so sure, and he didn't like what he saw forming overhead.

The gradual climb up the mountain and into mountain valleys brought changes in scenery, vegetation and weather. Lodge Pole Pines at the lower elevations replaced the sagebrush and greasewood of the prairie. As they climbed higher, spruce and firs replaced the pines and the air smelled fresh and cool.

The cooler air of the higher elevations were a welcome respite from the hot months crossing the prairie, but with the cooler air came problems. The warm air from the plains meeting the colder air of the mountains created thunderheads and rain usually followed. If the rains started they would not only wash out the trail they were following, but also their back trail. The three could well get lost in these wilderness mountains, as indeed, they may already be.

Johnny could find directions by reading the stars and the sun, but with clouds over head he would be blind both day and night. They could walk in circles for days.

Johnny was about to call Picker and Mathias to meeting to discuss ending the search when Picker hollered from a short distance ahead. "Johnny!"

Riding up to meet him Johnny answered, "Yeah, Picker, you find somethin'?"

"Fresh horse dung. Not more den half a day old, Johnny. Dey not too far ahead."

"We don't want to walk headlong into the middle of their camp. It'll soon be dark. Let's make camp. No fire," Johnny looked overhead at the cumulus clouds, "and hope the rain holds off."

The cooler days brought colder nights. For the first time the boys made use of the buffalo hides the Lakota Sioux had given them. They took advantage of the

Spruce branches and used them for bedding against the hard ground and covered themselves with the hides.

They weren't long asleep before the thunderstorm began. It didn't start far off in the distance as it had out on the prairie, but roared through the tall pines overhead splintering some and crashing them to the ground. Unlike prairie storms, there was no waiting for this storm to pass. Storms on the slopes of mountains begin as the elements present themselves and end as those elements dissipate. There was nothing to do but pray the trees they lay under were spared.

Johnny, lying a few feet from Mathias, heard him begin to whimper in fear. When the next crash of lightning ripped through the trees high over head, Mathias screamed, "Johnny!"

"The Lord," Johnny answered him, "Call out to the Lord, Mathias. Call out His name, not mine. There's nothin' I can do to help. The Lord didn't bring this storm on, the elements He set in motion millenniums ago did that, but He can keep you from bein' hurt by it if you ask."

"Stuff it, Farrell!" Mathias shouted.

Johnny grinned in the darkness in spite of his own fear. Another bolt of lightning tore open a tree not far away. Mathias whimpered again.

"All's you gotta do is ask, Mathias," Picker added.

The next bolt struck the top of a pine directly overhead, bringing all three off the ground. The flash temporarily blinded Johnny even though his eyes were closed. He was just about to call out to the Lord himself when a commanding shout from Mathias cut through the rumble of the thunder. Johnny saw, in the faint light of a burning fir tree nearby, the silhouette of Mathias, sitting up with his fist raised toward the heavens.

"Awright now God that's about enough! I know you're up there playin' with us like we was some kinda dumb yokels! You stop this now b'fore somebody gets hurt! Now! I say. Now!"

The thunder and lightning abated, silence fell around them. The three listened and waited.

"M'gosh," Mathias mumbled.

"Good show, Mathias," Johnny said. "Not exactly a church goin' prayer, but whatever works, I say. Right, Picker?"

"Ah d'clare," Picker said, giggling, "Ah not ever see a prayer answered dat fast. You done commanded dah heavens, Mathias."

"Ain't no denyin' it, his prayer was sincere," Johnny said, folding up in laughter.

As they all lay beneath their buffalo hides laughing, the rain began. First lightly, then a heavy downpour.

"Yeah," Mathias said, "now He's gonna drown us."

"Don't worry, Mathias. He don't want you yet, you're too onry."

"Not only dat," Picker added, "He scared to death of you."

The rain hissed in the burning fir tree and the three boys pulled their buffalo hides over them and tried for sleep.

★★★★★

Johnny opened his eyes the next morning and looked up expecting to see the tops of the trees and blue sky, but he saw neither. The fluffy cotton clouds he had seen from a distance while on the prairie were now all around them. The pony tracks they had been following were washed away in both directions. So intent on following the pony tracks, Johnny had forgotten to keep his bearings. Now he had no idea which direction east and south were--the route of return. They were hopelessly lost, he knew, and it was just a matter of time before Picker and Mathias would come to the same conclusion. He didn't hurry the moment.

Pushing aside his buffalo hide, Johnny gathered up the dry spruce branches he had used as bedding. He piled them up and set fire to them and piled more dead branches on top. He soon had a good fire going. He wasn't afraid of the Indians finding them now, indeed, they may be the only hope of finding their way back. He was convinced the Manley train survivors were better off with the Indians and his efforts now would be to bring Picker, Mathias and himself out of the mountain wilderness. The salt cured buffalo meat the Lakota Sioux had given them was running low.

The animals were still tethered to trees where they had left them the night before. Johnny retrieved the lead molds from the pack mule and withdrew the twisted lead balls from his pouch. He would melt them down and mold more lead balls. He had seen signs of deer on the way up. With luck I can kill a deer for us, he thought. He looked to the edge of the fog, he realized he would be unable to get close to a deer. His only hope would be to find a place to sit and wait for the deer to come to him.

Mathias and Picker were frying strips of buffalo meat over the fire when Johnny secured his powder horn and lead ball pouch in his belt and headed away from camp. Picker and Mathias had seen him head out on a hunting foray many times and had no reason to question him now and went about their business.

Johnny was a mile or so up a small trail when he saw fresh track that had been made since the rains of the night before. He was astonished at the size of these tracks. They looked like deer, but were much bigger, and the toes were far apart. Elk? He wondered. This brought to mind the bull elk he had seen on the cliff by the Allegheny River and the wolves that killed it. The wolves were hungry and following their natural instincts when they killed the elk. Now Johnny was about to do the same thing and for the same reason.

Following the tracks would be futile he knew, but at least in finding tracks he had hope. He found himself a comfortable hiding place under a fir tree in the undergrowth of laurel and fern near the trail.

A large creek, swollen by the recent rain, whispered as it meandered through the trees and thickets a short distance below. He waited. The success of a hunter, he thought, rests in the patience he has to lay in wait for his prey.

The hours went by and Johnny was about to give up hope. The short distance the fog allowed him to see all around, showed him little promise of an elk walking into his sights.

Suddenly, he heard a faint sound up the trail. He sat still, listening. May have just been imagining it, he thought. Your mind plays tricks on you after hours of lying in wait. There, he heard it again. A rustling in the leaves maybe, no. A pine branch scraping, what, "Hide?" he said in a whisper. Footsteps, faint. Coming closer. Still can't see anything. Dern fog. He could tell now the direction from which the noise was coming. He raised his rifle sighting down the barrel. The excitement of the kill began to form in his being. The feeling, he imagined, the mountain lion had just before it pounced, or the wolf before it attacked. Beads of perspiration began to form over his brow. It itched a little, but he couldn't make a sudden move to correct it. Not now. The elk was about to walk into his view. He could hear his own breathing, imagined it was awful loud, tried to stifle it, knew it was impossible. There, a figure began to form in the fog. Johnny held his breath as his father had taught him. Hold your breath, steady your aim just before you squeeze the trigger.

"Awwh?" Johnny gasped. What he saw, looking down the barrel, made him freeze his finger on the trigger and ease off. The tension drained from his body as a horse and rider came into view. It was an Indian. It wasn't a Lakota Sioux, he knew.

The Indian stopped his pony. Johnny remained hidden, not sure what this Indian's intentions were. The Indian turned in his buffalo hide saddle and made a jester behind him, saying something in his language.

From out of the fog came a sight that astounded
Johnny and his gasp almost gave away his position. A
young girl, white, maybe twelve, Johnny guessed, her
long calico dress in tatters, walked forward. Following
her was a young boy, a little smaller than Mathias, and a
little chubby, wearing spectacles. Johnny recognized him
as Charles William Fulbright the third. Behind him came
the girl with the curls Johnny now knew as Becky
Fergeson, her long white dress dirty and torn. Another
figure, walked out of the fog. Johnny guessed that must
be Manpreet Coonwaller. The good-looking features and
copper skin of his Indian heritage peered from under a
wide brimmed hat, but didn't mask an arrogant look
Johnny did not like. He wore an oversized vest that hung
lopsided on his thin but tall frame. Behind Manpreet
came three mounted warriors with bow in hand.

Johnny waited in hiding, wondering. Were they
about to kill them? No, they wouldn't do that. Then he
thought of the massacre of the Manley train. He raised
his rifle and felt for his powder horn and lead, placing
wads in his mouth in case he would have to fire in rapid
session. Did he have enough lead, he wondered? How
many Indians were back there in the fog?

The lead Indian pointed down the trail from which
Johnny had come and to where Mathias and Picker were
encamped. He said something to the children in broken
English Johnny did not understand, but the children ap-
parently did. The children started walking down the trail.
Charles turned and waved to the Indian.

The Indian waved back, then turned his pony and disappeared into the fog followed by the others.

Chapter Nineteen

THE REUNION

The survivors of the Manley train walked down the trail towards Picker and Mathias. Johnny stepped out of his hiding place onto the trail not far behind them.

"Ahem." He cleared his throat, hoping not to frighten them.

They turned to see Johnny with his rifle cradled in his arms.

Charles spoke up first. "You must be Johnny," he said.

Johnny was taken by surprise. "Now how did you know that?"

"The Indians told us you were following them and we would find you camped down this trail. That rifle gave you away. You are quite well known among the Indians for how well you use that rifle. You killed a big grizzly I understand. I must say, you do look familiar."

"Yes, we met briefly in Independence before the Manley train pulled out."

"Oh yes," Charles said with hurt in his voice and eyes, "ages ago it seems now."

Johnny looked at Becky Fergeson. She wasn't the same girl he saw aboard the *Mary Louise* and in Independence. She looked haggard and much older. "We met briefly too in Independence and on the steamboat *Mary Louise*," he said to her. "I understand your name is Becky. My name is Johnny. Pleased to meet you."

She said nothing, staring at the ground as she had been.

"She has been like that since . . . well since . . ." Charles couldn't say it.

"Yeah," Manpreet said with an arrogant tone in his voice Johnny did not like. "She's been mopin' like that since her parents got shot up."

"Keep your mouth shut, Manpreet," Charles insisted.

"Shut your own mouth, Pudgy Charlie," Manpreet dragged out the name, "or I'll grind those specks under my foot."

"My name is Sarah," the younger girl spoke up with a gleam in her eye not having taken her eyes off Johnny. "Sarah Jacobs. We left my baby sister with the Indians."

"With the Indians! Why?" Johnny asked of Charles.

"They had a wet nurse, we don't. The baby would have died of starvation with us. Sarah understands that, don't you Sarah?" Charles asked of Sarah.

"Yes, I think so," she shied away.

"Yeah, I was gettin' mighty tired of hearin it bawlin' anyhow," Manpreet said. "I was gettin' ready to strangle it."

"Our camp is just up ahead," Johnny said, looking sideways at Manpreet. As they started down the trail, he added, "Mathias will be happy to see you, Charles."

"Mathias Tibbs?" Charles asked, excited, "he's alive?"

"Yep," Johnny assured him, "alive and onry as ever."

Charles laughed. "That's Mathias all right! Does he give you trouble from time to time?"

"More often than not," Johnny said.

"He must like you," Charles replied.

"Well, that's hard to figure sometimes."

Johnny saw the glow of the campfire through the fog. In a few minutes they stepped, like ghosts, out of the misty cloud one by one. Mathias and Picker, standing by the fire, stiffened in shock until Mathias recognized Charles.

"Charlie!" Mathias hollered and the two ran and embraced each other.

"How many times do I have to tell you my name is Charles? Bad enough I have to put up with that from Manpreet."

"Oh, Manpreet," Mathias said with disgust, knowing Manpreet was within earshot "I was hopin' the Indians got him. Oh, hello Manpreet."

"The word is hoping, not hopin'," Charles said adjusting his spectacles.

"Don't start in on me, Charles, I swear."

Mathias gave his salutations to Sarah and Becky, though Becky did not acknowledge him. He then introduced Picker.

Picker wanted to thank Becky for what she had done for him on the steamboat but he could tell by looking at her there was something terribly wrong.

"What's wrong with Becky?" Mathias asked Charles.

"She has had a terrible time. Cholera took her mother first and the Indians killed her father," Charles replied.

"Yeah, Charles," Johnny interjected. "What happened back there?"

"I'll tell you all about it, but first we are famished. Would you have a bit of food for us?"

"Oh yes, of course," Johnny answered.

"We have some buffalo steaks Ah can cook over dah fire fo' you," Picker offered.

"That would be delightful." Charles said to Picker in a condescending manner. To Johnny he said, "Thank you."

They all sat around the fire and Charles, after removing his spectacles and cleaning them on the tail of his shirt, replaced them, wrapping the wire frames around his big ears. Johnny hadn't noticed his ears before, his hair growing over them. Charles then proceeded with his story of the tragic events on the trail as well as he understood them, both from what he saw and what the Indians later told him.

The Indians had come into camp to do some trading with the folks on the wagon train. This was not unusual as they had traded with the emigrants many times in the past with no trouble, although there is always tension on both sides. Whites and Indians not fully trusting one another. It seems that one of the menfolk of the train traded a bottle of whiskey for a pony. The Indian set the bottle of whiskey on the tailgate of the man's wagon and went to fetch the pony. When he returned, he handed over the pony to the fellow but when he went to get his whiskey it was gone. An argument ensued and somebody fired a shot, then the Indians let loose with a barrage of arrows. It was all over in a few seconds. Captain Manley, with an arrow in his chest, herded the younger children under a wagon and took up position to hold off an attack. The attack never came and Captain Manley expired. Soon the Indians came slowly back into the wagon circle to take what they could and found the young ones under the wagon.

"It was all a big misunderstanding of sorts," Charles added.

"The Indians took us with them because they new we would starve on the prairie. It all happened so fast. The whites fired first. They were not very good with a rifle though. They didn't hit anybody but the loud report of the rifles sent the Indians into action. It all happened so fast," Charles repeated.

Charles stopped. He took a deep breath to recover his composure, then continued. "Mother and Father were both killed there before my eyes. I should hate the Indians, I suppose.

"The Indians were afraid, so they took us and headed for the mountains. When they discovered you were on their trail they became fearful because of the story they heard about you."

"Are those Indians Sioux?" Johnny asked.

"I don't know," Charles answered. "It was quite difficult at first. They speak little English, but they were able to use signs with their broken English and we soon understood enough."

"Well, when the military finds out they have a white baby captive they will go after 'em," Johnny ventured.

"The baby is not a captive, Johnny. You have got to make sure the military understands that. The Indians didn't want the baby, they have babies of their own. They didn't want the baby to die," Charles pleaded.

"I understand that, Charles," Johnny said, "but somehow I don't think the military will look at it that way. Remember, you have Sarah here who is going to want her sister back someday."

"Yeah," Manpreet spoke up, "and I don't see things the way you do, Pudgy. They killed my pa. The Indians started the fight by tryin' to cheat ol' man Pendergras then they slaughtered everybody and took everything they could carry away, including us who they intended on making slaves until Johnny happened along."

"That is nonsense, Manpreet," Charles defended his explanation. "They could have easily out-distanced Johnny. They slowed down so Johnny could catch up. The Indians wanted to get rid of you. Anyhow, how do I know you didn't kill your father yourself, you were always threatening to."

"Here, here," Mathias spoke up. "I heard that a time or two myself, Coonwaller."

"It is true," Johnny interrupted, "we would never have been able to find them after that rain came and washed out the trail last night," Johnny added. "We were ready to give up the search. I'm sure they knew that."

"Sure they knew that," Charles replied. "Why is it so difficult for you to see the truth, Manpreet."

"That is the truth as I see it," Manpreet said, "and the story I will tell the military. They are murderers and have a captive white baby with them. The military will hunt them down like dogs."

There was silence among them for a few minutes each in his own way imagining the military action.

Then Johnny spoke up. "Well, that doesn't seem to be a concern of ours at the moment. What we have to worry about is gettin' out of these mountains alive. I gotta tell you all the truth. I haven't a notion about where we are or how we got here. The rain last night has changed things a bit. Trails are washed out and trees have fallen. I can't see the sun for clouds and fog so I don't know north from south, east from west. As near as I can figure, it is mid-September. The weather is getting colder and the snows will soon start up here. We have three warm buffalo hides. We will have to double up at night. The girls can use my hide, I'll double up with Picker. Mathias and Charles can double up and oh, Manpreet, I forgot about you.

Tell you what, Manpreet. Me, you and Picker will take turns standing guard all night since we are the oldest. That will leave two in the hide. Ain't no room for more than two."

"Isn't room," Charles interjected.

"What?" Johnny asked.

"The correct sentence should be, 'There isn't room for more than two.' There is no such word in the English language as 'ain't', Johnny."

"There ain't?" Johnny asked.

"There isn't," Charles answered.

"Then why do people use it?" Johnny asked

"Because they ain't literate," Mathias broke in, "Right Charles?"

"Aren't literate," Charles pushed his spectacles up on his nose and rolled his eyes in disgust.

"Well, if there ain . . . isn't no such word as "ain't" then I'll by golly not use it. Simple as that," Johnny agreed.

"Good heavens," Charles said, raising his hands in defeat, "a double negative. Such slaughter of the King's English I am hearing."

"I think you'll find it ain . . . isn't that easy, Johnny," Mathias said, "but with Charles doggin' your English trail you'll soon be wishin' it was or lookin' for a tree to hang him from."

"You ended your sentence with a preposition again, Mathias," Charles corrected.

"Stuff it, Charlie," Mathias retorted.

"Tsk, tsk," Charles replied, "You'll never learn proper English with that attitude."

"My English is proper enough. You understand me don't you Johnny?" Mathias asked.

"Well, your English I understand. You on the other hand puzzle me some."

Charles doubled over in laughter.

"How 'bout you, Picker. You understand me?" Mathias asked.

"Every bit, Mathias. Every bit," Picker answered with a chuckle.

Johnny enjoyed the exchange. He saw an opportunity for some fun and couldn't resist. "What's a preposition, Charles?" he asked.

"Oh no, Johnny," Mathias pleaded, "don't get him started."

"I'm glad you asked, Johnny. Shows you have interest in the finer things. A preposition is a word like 'in', 'to', 'by', 'from', 'at' that connects a noun or pronoun to another word. By it's very definition one should know not to use it at the end of a sentence," Charles glowered at Mathias.

"That makes sense," Johnny agreed. "What's a noun or pronoun?"

"Aaaaaaaah, noooo," Mathias shouted. "You answer that Charlie and I'm gonna ruin your day right here and now," Mathias threatened, waving a fist under Charles' nose.

"My name is what?" Charles said coolly.

"Charles," Mathias corrected.

"Looks like the English lesson is over for now, Johnny. Another time maybe?"

"Sure," Johnny agreed with humor in his voice. He wanted to get the subject back to their predicament. He wasn't sure they grasped the seriousness of the situation. They did not seem to be worried. Then he realized, they had placed all their confidence in him. So, he thought, time to throw the question out there and see what kind of answers I get.

"Does anybody here know the way outta these mountains?"

There was dead silence as the six of them sat stunned, staring at Johnny as if he had just ask the dumbest question in the world.

Johnny gazed into the fire and mumbled, "Just thought I'd ask."

Chapter Twenty

THE BULL ELK

The early hours of morning seemed unusually cold though the fog had lifted some. Johnny wondered if there was a snow storm threatening overhead. A bit early for that, he thought, but then weather has a way of changing very quickly in the mountains. The thoughts gave him a shiver as he worked his muscles to a start.

Their supplies of meat were getting dangerously low and they now had four more mouths to feed. They would need more meat before an attempt was made to find their way down the mountain when the weather cleared. It was time for him to hunt for whatever game he could find. Johnny prepared the water bag and packed several strips of jerky to take with him.

Sarah Jacobs had begged him to take her along, but he told her he would take her another time that it was important he go alone this time. She was disappointed, but accepted Johnny's reasoning.

Johnny threw some more pine branches on the fire and stood back as they flared up, sizzled and popped. The rain up here is as cold as icicles, he thought. Going to have to keep this fire going for warmth.

Satisfied the fire would maintain until the others woke up, he took up his rifle, powder horn and lead. He loaded the muzzleloader, except for the cap, then walked up the trail a mile or so to his hiding place in the fern and laurel.

The foliage of the underbrush was trimmed in ochre and, looking down towards the creek, Johnny could see the faint colors of autumn in the trees. Sitting motionless under the pine tree, he wished he had the buffalo hide to keep warm. He could smell the cold edge of winter on the wind. He placed the percussion cap over the hammer nipple and settled down to wait.

The hours dragged by.

Johnny had to readjust his sitting position to keep his legs from cramping. He reached into his pouch to retrieve some jerky. Chewing on jerky not only satisfied his hunger, but it also helped break the monotony. Chewing jerky took time and he had plenty of it. Having the patience to wait in hiding while hunting was always difficult for him. He found himself easily discouraged and had to fight the impulse to get up and move to a different location, but he kept telling himself this was as good a location as any other. Just be patient.

The jerky had left a good taste in his mouth and plenty of saliva. He took two load wads from his pocket, placing them on either side of his mouth.

Suddenly, a large figure moved casually out of the fog breaking off branches and chewing them as it walked through the high brush and trees off the trail to Johnny's left.

It was an elk. Wisps of steam emanated from its mouth and nose as it chewed.

Johnny slowly shifted his position to one knee on the ground and the other raised as a steady brace for his left elbow. The Hawkens resting in his left hand, he cautiously raised the rifle to his right shoulder and took aim. Looking down the barrel, he placed the sight on the animal and waited.

His adrenalin began to flow. He was well camouflaged and downwind from the elk. He had time. He let the great animal get closer. It was a bull elk and it raised its large head and antlers, looking in Johnny's direction, chewing and taking in the remnants of the branch it had previously detached. Again it raised its head and broke off another branch higher in the tree.

It took two more steps and was now standing broadside to Johnny and lined up with the trunk of a pine tree.

Perfect, Johnny thought, and pulled the trigger.

The rifle recoiled against Johnny's shoulder. The bull elk stood for a few more seconds then dropped to it's knees before rolling on its side. Johnny quickly reloaded the Hawkens. He then pulled his knife from its scabbard as he ran to the elk. He pushed the blade into the elk's throat, severing its trachea. Then he walked over to the tree and found where the lead ball had entered. He dug it out, looked at it's twisted shape, flipped it into the air, caught it and dropped it into his pouch. He thought of Mathias and smiled.

Johnny gutted and skinned the elk where it lay, then began the process of dressing-out the animal, the warm blood soaking into the sodden earth. He wrapped freshly cut sections inside the hide. He would need one of the mules to haul those sections back to camp for Picker to salt cure. Very pleased with himself, he thought, this will feed us for some time.

He walked a short distance to the creek. He washed the blood off his hands and cleaned his knife. Taking up his rifle to return to camp, he turned to take a last glance at his morning's labor. Traces of steam rose from the still warm pile of meat. Movement beyond the creek caught his eye. He studied the brush but saw nothing. Must've been a bird flittering among the branches, he thought. He turned and made his way back to camp.

"Hey, Mathias!" Johnny hollered upon entering the camp perimeter. "Bring ol' Dan and Dave there. I've got a job for them."

There was immediate excitement in the camp at the news of the kill.

"You get a deer, Johnny?" Sarah asked. "Can I go back with you to fetch it?"

"You sure can, Sarah. Go get my mare and you can ride with me."

"Naw, I'll ride by myself. I'll take Pickers horse. Can I, Picker?" Sarah pleaded.

"Sho 'nuff, little girl," Picker agreed. "You can ride wid out a saddle?"

"Just you watch," Sarah said. Running to Pickers gelding she grasped the reins in one hand, placed both her hands tight on the startled horse's withers and flung herself up, skirt, petticoats and all.

Johnny and Picker both stood mouths agape as Sarah galloped the horse up to them.

A little embarrassed, Johnny said, "That's not very ladylike, Sarah."

"Baahh," Sarah admonished. "I ain't growed enough to be a lady yet. And even so, who says a lady can't ride a horse?"

"I haven't grown enough . . . ," Charles corrected.

"You ain't, Charles?" Sarah interrupted, anticipating the correction.

"No, I didn't say that . . ."

"Forget it Charles, you lost," Mathias interrupted leading the mules. "I'm ready when you girls are through lollygaggin'."

"We should be back in an hour or so, Picker. Got a big elk out there gonna take some saltin'. We got enough salt left?"

"Should be 'nuff," Picker answered.

"Good. Come on, Mathias. Sarah. Oh Charles, has Becky talked any yet?"

"Not yet. These things take time, Johnny."

"Yeah, guess you're right. Sure would feel better if she'd talk though. Gives me the shivers her starin' like that. Don't know what to do to help."

"Best thing to do is wait, Johnny," Charles said, "Sooner or later she will talk. I'll keep talking to her as I have been all along. I might just say the right thing or combination of things that will bring her alive."

"Thank you, Charles. You can give us all English lessons when we return," Johnny said.

"Oh don't encourage him, Farrell," Mathias moaned as he rode one of the mules up the trail and led the other.

Picker and Charles laughed and waved goodbye.

"Manpreet?" Johnny called. "Where's Manpreet, Charles? He has late watch tonight he'll need to get some rest."

"I don't know. He walked out into the woods a while ago. I assumed he had a natures call. I let him be."

Johnny nodded acknowledgment to Charles then reined his mare around.

"Come on, Johnny," Sarah said. "You want to race."

"No point in tuckering out the horses, Sarah," Johnny said. "Ain't no contest anyhow, this mare against that big gelding. I've already seen the results. Besides, we've got to wait for ol' poky back there with the mules."

"Don't you fret none, Farrell," Mathias spoke up. "You ain't traveled an inch farther on that horse than I have on this mule."

"No, but I traveled a sight faster," Johnny argued.

"Now if that don't make sense," Mathias shot back. "How come if you traveled faster, you ain't no farther than me, no sooner?"

"Mathias, you'd argue with the Lord Hisself if He offered you the keys to His Kingdom," Johnny said.

"No, I'd just ask him if there was anybody by the name of Farrell in there first," Mathias laughed.

"Well, that's mighty kind of you to consider I would be in there, Mathias," Johnny returned.

"No, I didn't say you in particular, I said 'anybody' by the name of Farrell."

"Give it up, Johnny," Sarah said. "Sounds like your losin' this one."

"Seems I lose them all with him," Johnny said.

They arrived at the location on the trail where Johnny's hiding place was in the underbrush down by the creek.

"Is this the place, Johnny?" Mathias yelled. "I ain't never seen a elk before. Where's it at?" Mathias got off the mule and walked into the trees and bushes a ways.

"Well, Mathias, there ain't a lot to look at now. It's all cut up in pieces down there in that brush by the creek. The head and antlers are a sight to see though."

"Good, I'll go fetch them up here," Mathias said as he started down through the brush.

Sarah and Johnny had just dismounted when they heard Mathias shouting at something or someone down by the creek.

"Hey, get away from that!" he shouted. "That ain't yours! Get away!"

Johnny and Sarah looked at one another. Then, of a sudden, Johnny realized what he may have seen moving in the bushes earlier.

"Hold these horses here, Sarah," he commanded, then ran down through the bushes, rifle in hand, instinctively placing load wads in his mouth.

He came within view of the creek and saw Mathias shouting and waving at a black bear that was gorging itself on the elk. It growled at Mathias, but for the most part ignored him.

Johnny inwardly smiled at Mathias' defiance, but when he saw Mathias reach inside his vest his blood ran cold. He shouted in terror. "Noooo, Mathias, don't!"

Whether Mathias didn't hear him or paid him no mind Johnny didn't know. The events that followed happened in seconds. Mathias pulled out his derringer, shot at the bear. The bear became enraged, stood up on its hind legs and swung its forepaw, catching Mathias on the side of the head.

Mathias came off his feet and disappeared into the underbrush. Johnny quickly shouldered his rifle and fired. The bear also disappeared into the brush. Johnny quickly reloaded the rifle, listening. There was no noise, no motion from the thick undergrowth.

Johnny walked quietly toward the creek and the remains of the elk. Pushing the branches away, he listened for any noise that would tell him of Mathias or the bear. He tensed up expecting the bear to charge out of the thickets. Slowly, he eased up near the pile of elk remains that were now strewn about.

"Johnny!" Sarah shouted from the trail above, "Where are you? What's going on? What did you shoot at?"

Johnny didn't answer her. Couldn't. Didn't want to give away his position. He crouched low in the branches, moving forward. His eyes penetrated the thick foliage, looking for movement or signs of blood on the ground or leaves.

"Jon-neee!" Sarah shouted again.

Johnny knew Sarah was frightened. Wished he could answer her. Stay on the trail with the animals, he wanted to shout back at her. Don't come into the woods there may be a wounded, crazed bear ready to bounce on the first movement it sees or scent it picks up. He slowly raised his left arm and pushed a small branch from his path. Took a light step forward being certain not to place his foot on a dead branch. One snap of a branch is all it would take. Cautiously, he moved forward.

Then he saw blood.

The wide leaves of the Rocky Mountain Maple, beginning to turn color for its autumn display, yielded the crimson color of blood running down it's veined leaf. Johnny took another step, pushing aside a branch. There on the mossy ground in front of him lay Mathias. "Oohhh," he groaned, for he knew Mathias was dead. Knew his neck was broken. Johnny wanted to run to him, but couldn't.

He looked around. The leaves of the maple swayed gently on the breeze.

Suddenly, Johnny heard movement. Faint at first, coming from the direction of the trail.

"John-neee!" Sarah called. She was coming into the underbrush. "Where are you?"

Johnny felt a sharp sting of fear surge through him. "Sarah!" he hollered. "No, don't come down here! Go back!"

Then he heard the snapping of branches and saw the enraged bear crashing through the brush a distance away. The bear must have circled around when Sarah first hollered, moving toward her. Now he stopped, seemed confused. Sniffed the air in the direction of Sarah who was now well into the undergrowth, working her way toward Johnny.

Johnny sensed the bear's intention. He began to run toward the bear, hollering as he went to bring the bears attention to him and away from Sarah. But it wasn't working. The bear had her scent and ran up the slope in her direction.

Sarah must have seen the bear before it saw her. As Johnny followed the progress of the bear, he caught a glimpse of Sarah climbing a tree. She was out of the bears reach when it arrived, growling and snorting. The bear grasped the trunk of the tree and began to shake and bend it.

Sarah could have picked a better tree, Johnny thought.

Running through the brush Johnny heard Sarah scream. "Johnnee!"

"I'm comin' Sarah, hold on!" Johnny hollered. He reached a clearing big enough to see the bear and the tree but couldn't see Sarah. He was dangerously close. He knew he had to make this shot count. He raised the rifle, took careful aim, and fired. The bear let out a loud roar, whirled around and glared with red eyes at Johnny.

Johnny had little time to reload. He scrambled for his powder horn and lead. Nervously he fumbled with the powder, spilling most of it, not knowing how much entered the barrel. He removed the wad from his mouth, pushed it down the barrel with the lead ball, but he lost the rhythm--forgot where he was. Powder, wad 'n . . . wad 'n . . . He removed a second wad from his mouth, packed it in with another lead ball and rammed it tight with the rod, then placed the cap. The bear advanced fast.

Johnny hadn't had the time to raise the rifle to his shoulder. When the bear pushed its huge chest against the rifle barrel, Johnny pulled the trigger. He saw a great flash. Heard the roar of the wounded animal. Smelled burned flesh and hair. Felt burning pain in his right arm and side. He never felt the ground come up to meet him, or the weight of the bear upon him.

Chapter Twenty-One

THE REVELATION

The bear lay in his own blood, a crumpled heap, at Johnny's side. In a daze, Johnny pulled himself up and rested on his left elbow. A gaping, blood-clotted wound ran from his right hand up his arm. His shirt hung in tatters over the powder burns that ached below his right ribcage.

When his head cleared Johnny pulled himself to his feet and staggered down to the creek. He splashed water on his face and cleaned the blood from his hand and wrist, opening the wound. He ripped at his shirt until he had a piece of cloth big enough to use as a bandage. He steadied himself, trying to bring into focus the events that brought him here.

He looked toward the underbrush where he had seen Mathias. He walked over and found his body. He listened for a heartbeat, hoping, but none was there. He shook his head, feeling hopeless.

"I should've known," he said. "I failed to protect you, Mathias. I shouldn't of let you come down here by yourself. God forgive me. I failed this boy."

Turning towards the tree in which he last saw Sarah he hollered, "Sarah!"

He walked back up the hill to where the bear lay and noticed, protruding from underneath the bear, the shattered stock of the rifle. He pulled the rifle from under the bear, looked at the split barrel and threw it down in disgust.

"Breached," he said, "I'm lucky to be alive." He looked down at the bear and realized it had taken the brunt of the blast.

"Sarah!" he hollered again but got no answer. The tree that Sarah had climbed was almost uprooted, but Sarah was nowhere in sight.

Johnny walked up to the trail and found the animals were gone. Feeling weak, he sat down in the middle of the trail and tried to sort things out. Then he heard the pounding of hoofbeat coming up the trail. It was Sarah on the gelding followed by Picker on the mare.

"Johnny!" Sarah hollered as she came off the back of the gelding in full stride. She ran up to Johnny and flung her arms around him. "You're alive! I thought you were dead." She began to sob, "I saw you under that bear all covered with blood, I thought you were dead."

Johnny looked at Picker, who wore the look of a very frightened boy. Picker looked at Johnny's arm and blood soaked clothes.

"Looks to be you wrestled dat bear to dah ground, Johnny. You hurtin' anywheres else?"

For the first time Johnny looked at his clothing. They were soaked in the blood of the bear. Still a little dazed he said, "No, I don't think so. Got powder burns on my side. The rifle's no good no more, Picker. It's all my fault."

Picker looked around, "Where's Mathias?" he asked.

"Mathias?" Johnny asked. Then a great weight descended up him. He brought his hands to his face. "Mathias. Oh God, Mathias. He's dead, Picker. Mathias is dead. The bear killed him. He's down there in the brush. He shot the bear with that derringer. It was like a bee sting to the bear. Made him mad. That foolish boy, that foolish, foolish boy."

"Po' Mathias," Picker said, "Ah go an' fetch him up. Po' Mathias."

"I'll go with you, Picker," Johnny suggested. "I know where he is. Sarah you stay with the horses."

"I'm happy you're not dead, Johnny," Sarah said, "but I'm sad 'bout Mathias. I'm scared Johnny. What's gonna happen to us?"

"Everything's gonna be fine, Sarah," Johnny assured her. "Stay by the horses now."

They brought Mathias up to the trail. Picker mounted his gelding and Johnny handed Mathias up to him.

Stricken with grief, Picker rode back to camp with Mathias cradled in his arms. Johnny rode back on the mare with Sarah behind him.

It was a sorrowful procession as they rode into camp. Sarah had brought word that Johnny had been the one who was dead so Charles and Manpreet were surprised to see Johnny alive. Charles, however, grew near hysterics when he saw Mathias hanging limp in Pickers arms.

"Mathias?" he cried out. "What has happened to you?"

"He dead, Charles," Picker said and broke down in sobs, "dah bear kilt him."

Suddenly there was a scream from across the camp. It was Becky. "Charles!" she shouted. "Is Mathias dead? Too much dyin', Charles. We're all gonna die, I see it in my dreams."

She became hysterical and began beating her fists into the ground. Charles ran over to her and held her hands. She fell into his arms sobbing. "I have bad dreams, Charles. Terrible dreams. We're all gonna die."

Johnny reached around with his left arm, lowered Sarah to the ground, leaped from the mare and ran to Becky. "Everything's gonna be fine, Becky" he said. "Everything's gonna be fine." He suddenly realized he had said the same thing to Sarah and wasn't sure he believed it himself. Though they had meat now in the bear and elk, they no longer had the rifle. They were at the mercy of the elements and without protection.

"I want to go to San Francisco!" Becky murmured.

Johnny looked at Charles who shrugged his shoulders.

"You want to go to San Francisco?" Johnny asked, wanting to be sure of what he heard.

Her gaze fixed upon the ground in front of her, Becky nodded her head slowly. "I want to perform on stage like Lola Montez. I saw her in New York. She is beautiful and has a wonderful voice. She is somewhere in California now."

"Sounds like a very nice dream," Johnny said. "Dreams are what keep us goin' in life, tryin' to make them come true." He recalled what the Irishman had told him on the *Mary Louise*. " 'Tis a fine thing to have a dream."

The girl did not respond to Johnny. He began fidgeting with his hat brim. "Sometimes we can't fulfill our dreams by ourselves though," he said, "we need others to help us along the way."

Becky looked at Johnny now. "Would you help me?" she asked.

"Sure, that's what I'm tryin' to do." Johnny looked heavenward and saw that the clouds were breaking up. Patches of blue sky poked through white rolling clouds. "I'm tryin' to get you back to Fort Laramie."

"No," she said, "help me get to California."

"California? Oh, I'm afraid it's too late in the season for that. Going to have to wait 'til next spring. Snow storms will be starting soon in the mountains."

Johnny felt the Dreamcatcher beneath his shirt. He removed it from around his neck. He looked upon it for the last time and placed it around Becky's neck.

Becky took up the Dreamcatcher in her hands and looked at it. Her eyes brightened.

Johnny explained it's meaning. "Mebbe it will take away your bad dreams and help make your good dreams come true," he said.

Becky smiled at Johnny then looked upon the Dreamcatcher that lay in the palms of her hands. Soon the smile faded and she returned to staring at the ground before her.

Johnny knew the conversation had ended. There was nothing more he could do to help her. He raised himself off the ground, nodding to Charles. Then he watched as Picker lay Mathias gently on the ground a sort distance away, covering him with one of the buffalo hides. Picker walked over to Johnny.

"Best you let me look at dat arm, Johnny," he said.

"Look up there, Picker!" he said. "The weather is breaking. By mornin' we can start down the mountain."

"Ah'll git a grave dug for Mathias before dark." Pickers spirits did not lift with the news. "Ah doin like buryin' him up here all by hisself."

"Picker, you got to understand somethin' about death," Johnny consoled. "We are only buryin' Mathias' body. Consider that he is with his ma and pa, not alone."

"Ah miss him, Johnny," Picker said.

"You miss his spirit, Picker. You miss his cantankerous humor. His goading me and Charles. I miss him too and Charles surely does, don't you, Charles?"

"Yes, I certainly do," Charles mumbled.

"Think of it though, Picker," Johnny continued. "Why, I'll bet he's right now banging on the Gates of Heaven with his fists demanding to be let in."

Picker chuckled at that. Then after thinking about it said, "Yup, an' Ah can hear him sayin', 'say, dere ain't nobody in dere by dah name of Farrell, is dere?'"

They laughed and their spirits were lifted until they looked over at the body.

"Come on, Picker," Johnny said, "I'll help you dig the grave. Where's Manpreet? I swear that fellow has a way of disappearin' when there's work to be done."

* * * * *

The clearing skies of the day before brought a very cold night and a colder morning. Johnny was up early building up the fire for breakfast, being eager to start down the mountain. Manpreet returned from the last watch of the night. Swinging his arms about he walked over and stood by the fire.

"Mornin' Manpreet," Johnny said. "Any trouble last night?"

"Nope. Had a time keepin' warm though. Good thing I had that bear hide."

"Yep, least somethin' good come of that tragedy," Johnny answered.

"Lot's of good the way I see it. Plenty of bear meat and one less mouth to feed."

Johnny felt his temper flare. He turned and took a step toward Manpreet, but before he could take another step Charles came from behind Manpreet and caught him around the mid-section. "I heard that, Manpreet," he shouted.

Picker and the girls followed closely behind. Johnny reached for Charles to pull him off Manpreet. He knew Manpreet would react furiously and Charles was no match. Before Johnny could respond Manpreet lost his balance, falling into the dirt near the fire. A bottle flew from his vest pocket. Charles quickly picked up the bottle and read the label.

"Whiskey!" Charles exclaimed.

"Whiskey?" Johnny asked in astonishment. "Where did you get that, Manpreet? It's half empty. Now I know why you turned up missing from time to time. You were off drinking whiskey."

At first Johnny saw humor in it, but looking at Charles and the girls the humor dissipated quickly. He sensed trouble.

"I know where he got it," Charles said.

"Yeah," Sarah and Becky said almost in unison.

"He stole it from the Indian," Charles continued. "It was the last bottle of whiskey Mister Pendergras had and he traded it for the pony. You caused the massacre of Manley's wagon train, you fool."

"You killed my father!" Becky screamed at him.

"And my ma and pa!" Sarah added. "And got my baby sister taken from me."

Manpreet sat on the ground in defiance. "I didn't kill nobody," he said. "The Indians killed 'em. You best watch from now on, Pudgy Charlie. I catch you by yerself an' I'll pound you into the ground. Spectacles, fat, an' all."

"Let's get the mules packed and start walking. It is late September, the sun is rising to the southeast. That is the direction we must go, to Fort Laramie." Johnny said.

Glaring at Manpreet, he poured the whiskey on the

ground. "Today is your lucky day, Manpreet. You roused my Irish temper. You can thank Charles for interferin'. Best you don't harm that boy whilst I'm around."

Charles, Becky and Sarah eased off though their eyes burned with anger at Manpreet who still sat on the ground.

Picker remained with Johnny and Manpreet. To Manpreet he said, "Mathias was mah friend. Never speak bad of him again."

They said their last goodbyes to Mathias and walked toward the rising sun. Sarah and Becky were mounted on the mare and gelding, leading the mules laden with their remaining supplies of meat and hides. Johnny kept Manpreet at a distance from the others, he wanted no trouble. He just wanted to get them to Fort Laramie. Possibly he and Picker could make it across the Sierra Mountains by themselves.

The Autumn sun lowered quickly behind the western forest. Johnny decided to camp for the night. No longer sure of his southeasterly march, he would wait for the rising sun.

A grumbling of anger and hostility toward Manpreet made Johnny decide to put him on first guard watch to keep him from agitating any more then he already had.

"Take first watch, Manpreet," Johnny instructed, "and wake Picker for the second watch. I'll take last watch. Take the bear hide with you, it's warmer."

Johnny built the fire up and they all laid in a circle around the fire with their feet toward the heat. The fire snapped and crackled, a sound that always made Johnny feel secure before falling off to sleep. Tonight, however, he was troubled at the events of the past couple of days and the changing attitude of the girls and Charles. He didn't remember going to sleep and was startled when Picker shook him violently to wake him in the early hours of morning.

"Fine, Picker, fine. I know it's my turn. You don't have to shake me to pieces!" Johnny complained.

"Hurry, Johnny," Picker whispered, "somethin's awful wrong." Picker pulled Johnny up. Johnny stumbled in the direction he was being pulled.

"What is it, Picker?" Picker kept pulling Johnny toward the camp perimeter where the guard was posted. Suddenly, he stopped and pointed down.

On the ground lay the heap of bear hide with Manpreet under it.

"He's sleepin' on duty? Well that's bad, but this ain't the military, Picker," Johnny complained.

"He ain't sleepin', Johnny. He dead," Picker whispered.

"Dead! Dead?" Johnny blurted out. "How? Indians?"

"His head bashed in with dat rock," Picker said, pointing at a rock that lay near Manpreets head. "He din't wake me for watch so Ah come lookin' for him, 'spectin' to find him asleep. I shook him den felt dah blood and saw dat rock in dah moonlight. Ah din't do dis, Johnny. Ah swear, Ah din't . . ."

"I know that, Picker. Indians didn't do it either. They would've used a knife and killed all of us in our sleep. Picker, one of those three layin' by that fire back there is a murderer."

"Or all three," Picker added.

Johnny could see the whites of Pickers wide eyes in the moonlight and remembered the fear he saw in him when aboard the *Mary Louise*. Johnny now felt the same fear. "We're goin' to have to watch each other's backs, Picker. They could just as well kill me an' you. Dead witnesses don't talk."

Chapter Twenty-Two

THE POLITICIAN

Johnny and Picker stood at the perimeter of the camp and watched as the fire burned low. Sarah, Charles and Becky lay by the fire seemingly undisturbed by the events of the night.

"They don't appear to be bothered by what they've done, Picker. They're sleeping like babies."

"Sho' doin figger, Johnny. Ah never would've thought dey do such a thing. Sho' doin figger."

"Those young'uns saw their folks murdered, Picker. They blamed Manpreet and took out their rage on him. I s'pose in a way he was responsible. Strange though, they never blamed the Indians."

"Po' Manpreet. He sho' picked a bad time to steal whiskey."

"There ain't no good time to steal, Picker." Johnny assured him. "From now on we don't stand guard against the Indians or anything else out there. We face into camp and keep a constant eye on those three. They spook me."

Johnny turned and looked toward the east. "Dawn is breaking. Let's go get that spade and get another grave dug, Picker."

"Ah's beginning to feel like a undertaker, Johnny."

"Look at the bright side, Picker. You know it ain't your grave you're diggin' if you're alive and well enough to dig it."

"You sho' have a way of liftin' mah spirits, Johnny."

Johnny sat on the ground at the campfire across from the three mounds of hide that were Charles, Becky and Sarah. Throwing more wood on the fire he looked at the three, knowing what he was about to encounter.

"Rise, children. We must talk," Johnny announced. The three mounds of hides moved slowly then all three sat up and stared at Johnny like he was some stranger who wandered into camp. The girls wore a look of fear and anger that penetrated Johnny's facade of courage. Charles' was a stare of . . . contempt, Johnny guessed, very unlike what he had come to know of him.

"Manpreet is dead!" Johnny blurted out. He was not surprised when there was no reaction or change of expression. Their stares were beginning to make Johnny feel ill-at-ease.

He made an attempt to get Sarah to talk. "Sarah," he said, "talk to me."

Sarah's eyes made a quick darting look sideways at Charles then back to Johnny, but she said nothing.

"Charles?" Johnny asked, but didn't expect an answer.

"Get yourselves up," Johnny announced. "Eat some vittles. Then the three of you will be walking the rest of the way. I will lead on my mare. Picker will bring up the rear on his gelding. Charles, you and Sarah will lead the mules."

With that said, Johnny walked off, agitated, feeling more spooked then before. Somethin's gone terribly wrong here, he thought.

Picker was hard at digging the grave when Johnny approached. "What dey say?" he asked.

"Not a word, Picker. They just stared at me. Gave me a bad case of the shivers. Darndest thing you ever seen. They don't even look the same. Like some evil thing has taken over their bodies. Let me have that spade, I gotta work off this . . . feeling."

"You sho' yo' arm is well 'nuff to dig, Johnny?" Picker asked.

"It does hurt some, but I'll be careful with it," Johnny answered.

"It goin' be a long journey to Fort Laramie dis way, Johnny. One good thing, dey have no weapons," Picker said.

Johnny looked back toward camp at the three figures standing about the fire with the hides draped over them. He touched his hand to the knife at his belt. "Well, they found a way to kill Manpreet, Picker. Like I said, we're going to have to watch each other's backs."

* * * * *

The trek down the mountain was slow going as the storms had downed trees and branches along the trails.

Weeks later while making camp by a small stream they refilled the water gourds and let the animals graze on the first signs of grass in the lower foothills. The three had still not spoken a word except to one another in guarded fashion. Johnny and Picker had grown accustomed to the silence and were paying less and less attention to them and to watching one another's backs.

Johnny was sitting by the stream deep in thought about the events of the past few weeks when, of a sudden, a strange feeling came over him; like he was being watched. He whirled around and there stood Sarah a short distance away.

At that moment Picker yelled from somewhere down the slope beyond the trees.

"Johnny! Johnny come here quick!"

Sarah gave Johnny a quick look then ran back toward the mules.

Johnny was immediately taken with fear and apprehension. Had they already done something to Picker? He ran down the slope in the direction of Picker's voice beyond the trees.

"Picker, where are you? What's wrong?" he shouted.

"Over here!"

Johnny saw Picker standing on a knoll, looking out over the prairie, but he saw none of the others. "Picker, what in . . . ? What are you yellin' about? You liked to scared me to shivers."

"Oh, sorry Johnny," he said. "Look dere." He pointed down to the south east.

"The prairie? Yup, we made it outta the mountains. Now we gotta figure out how far we are from the trail to Fort Laramie. I'm not sur . . ."

"No, Johnny. Not dah prairie, dah wagon. See dere?" Picker still pointed south east.

"Wagon? Mathias' wagon? Well I'll be . . . Geez you have good eyes, Picker. I'd of missed that for sure."

Down on the prairie floor a small black speck stood out against the light brown grass. "You brought us out good, Johnny. Right near dah wagon," Picker said.

"Just luck, Picker, or Divine Providence. Now we can back track our own trail. There ain't been no rain down here, I can see that.

"Sarah sneaked up behind me a bit ago, Picker. Gave me a start. Don't know what was on her mind. She ran off when you hollered. We haven't been keeping our eyes skinned on those three."

The next day, when they arrived at the wagon, they hitched the mules and loaded their dwindling supplies. Johnny had Sarah drive the wagon and Becky ride beside her. Sarah handled the wagon as good as she rode a horse. Johnny admired her for her abilities. She had been no trouble at all until events of the recent past. Johnny couldn't help thinking that somehow she was an unwilling partner in this troubled trio.

Becky had been going in and out of her strange episodes. Most often she wouldn't talk for days and when she did, it made no sense to anybody.

Charles walked beside the wagon keeping close to Sarah and Becky. Johnny noticed that Charles had lost a lot of weight since he had first seen him in Independence. Must be the short vittles and all the walking on the wagon trail. If it hadn't been for his suspenders his britches would be falling down, he thought.

Johnny got off the mare and led her behind the wagon, deciding walking wouldn't hurt him either.

The wheels of the wagon squealed for lack of grease and the board planking rattled from having set in the heat of the sun for months.

Johnny looked back at the foothills and noticed the colors of fall showing on the trees and shrubs. He studied the angle of the sun and his shadow on the ground. Must be gettin' close to October by now, he thought. He noticed how much the coat on his mare and the mules had grown. Gonna be a long cold winter.

Picker reined up behind the wagon, dismounted and joined Johnny. Sarah stopped the wagon on a rise that presented a view across the prairie. She climbed from the wagon bench to rest and stretch her legs.

"What you thinkin' 'bout Johnny?" Picker asked.

"What makes you think I'm thinkin' 'bout anything at all?" Johnny said.

"You always thinkin', Johnny. You have a good mind for thinkin'. You got us out of dose mountains. Got me off dat boat."

"Thank you, Picker, but if I was such a great thinker I wouldn't of got us in those mountains to begin with. Mathias would still be alive."

Charles spoke up from the front of the wagon, "And we would still be with the Indians, possibly for the rest of our lives. Sarah and Becky would have become wives of some braves, or worse. I think you did quite well. I must congratulate and thank you," he said as he walked to the rear of the wagon.

Johnny raised his head quickly at the sound of Charles' voice, astonished at what he said. He and Picker looked with surprise at each other.

"What brings you to say that, Mister Fulbright?" Johnny asked.

"It needed to be said. First I mean. Before I say what I am about to say."

"Oh?" Johnny threw a puzzled glance at Picker.

Sarah jumped back onto the bench of the wagon and took up the reins. The wagon had been blocking Johnny and Pickers view of the prairie beyond or they would have seen the column of mounted cavalry a mile or two away. Sarah slapped the reins across the mules behinds and the wagon lurched forward headed toward the column.

"Those soldiers," Charles said, pointing toward the column, "have no doubt discovered the massacre sight and are tracking the Indians who did it. Wouldn't you agree, Mister Farrell?"

"Yes, I would agree," Johnny answered, wondering where this was going. He looked at Picker who was alarmed at the column of soldiers advancing on them. His natural fear of authority, Johnny thought.

Sarah, Becky and the wagon were very near approaching the column.

"You might be wondering why Sarah and Becky are so anxious to reach those soldiers, Johnny," Charles stated.

"Yes, the thought has crossed my mind," Johnny replied, waiting to hear more.

"They have been living in fear of you since you killed Manpreet, Johnny," Charles said.

"What!" Johnny replied.

"Dat's not true," Picker retorted.

Charles ignored Picker's remark and, in fact, hardly acknowledged his presence.

Sarah and Becky had now caught up to the column.

"At this very moment they are telling the officer in charge of that column the whole story. From the massacre to Manpreet. They will tell him of their rescue from the Indians with your help, but they will also tell him you murdered Manpreet because he stole the whiskey that caused the massacre. That you considered yourself judge, jury and executioner. I am telling you this now so you can escape. You have fresh horses. Those soldiers have been traveling hard across the hot prairie. Their horses are tired."

"Why would those girls tell a lie like that, Charles?" Johnny asked.

"Because that is the way I told them the story. They trust and believe me," Charles replied.

Suddenly, facts and suspicions came together in Johnny's mind. "You killed Manpreet didn't you, Charles?" Johnny asked.

"Yes I did. I was extremely distraught that night, thinking of my parents and the way they died. I was also afraid of Manpreet and I hated him. I knew he would be sleeping while on guard so I took a rock from camp and bashed his head in with it. I am ashamed of what I did, but somehow, for some reason, I felt justified in doing it. To be honest, Johnny, I didn't have faith in the fact that we would ever get off that mountain alive. I firmly believed there would only be one of us left in the end and that would be Manpreet. He would have killed us all if it meant his survival. Just like the Donner party, he would have killed us for food. I saw him kill a camp dog and eat it once. He scared me. I feel justice has been served where Manpreet is concerned."

"Well I think a court of law in the states will decide that, Charles. I'll just tell my side of the story and Picker here will be my witness you confessed."

"In the first place a Negro slave will make a poor witness in the States, Johnny" Charles said in his condescending voice.

"Secondly, you will never make it to a court of law in the states. Those soldiers will hang you. This is a military matter out here. You see, Mathias told me all about you and . . . " Charles indicated toward Picker, " . . . the black. You were Mathias' hero, Johnny, and he bragged about how you escaped the law in Independence. Mathias was just a cut above a criminal himself, which is why he took to you.

"Thirdly, I am the son of Charles William Fulbright the second, a physician and scholar and very affluent. I am educated in the best schools in the States. I am privileged. Nobody is going to take your word over mine.

"I would guess that by now there is a wanted poster on you two hanging on the wall at Fort Laramie. A Negro and a White traveling together are easy to spot, and, that they would be wanted for murder is easy for simple minds to believe."

"Maybe there isn't a poster on us at all," Johnny suggested.

"There where quite a few people killed on that boat, Johnny." Charles reminded him.

"We had nothing to do with it, Charles," Johnny insisted.

Charles looked at Johnny and shrugged his shoulders. "I believe you, but that bunch won't," he said, pointing at the column. "Sarah is telling them all about you, just as Mathias told me, and I told her."

"You could fess up to it, Charles," Johnny suggested.

"What, and besmirch the Fulbright name. No, no, Johnny you don't understand. I am educated and am headed, possibly, for Oxford. I am destined for high political office. This country needs people like me to govern people like you. The Fulbright name must be protected at all cost. You will take the fall, Johnny. It's just the practical thing to do. Nothing personal."

Johnny looked to the column of soldiers. Two of them had separated from the column and started riding hard toward them.

"I will say my farewell now, Johnny." Charles said. "I suggest you . . . how would you say it, 'high tail it outta here'?"

"Tsk, Tsk, Charles, that is terrible English," Johnny said as he and Picker swung onto their mounts.

Charles walked in the direction of the column and the oncoming horsemen.

"What do you think of that boy, Picker?" Johnny said as they sat their mounts, watching the advance of the mounted pair.

"Not much," was the curt reply.

"He forgot something in his arrogance though. In the States you may not make a good witness, but out here it's another matter." Johnny withdrew the map from inside his shirt. "There is another garrison west of here called Fort Hall. We're going to find us a sympathetic ear and tell our side of this story to clear our names. Charles, however, will remain untouched I'm sure. I truly believe he will make a good politician someday. After all, we need people like him to govern people like us. Don't you agree?"

Picker looked at Johnny with furrowed brow, then looked with apprehension at the advancing soldiers.

Johnny said, "The last one to California is a slimy toad."

They reined their mounts around and heeled them to a fast gallop, the hooves throwing up clumps of dry prairie sod.

The two pursuing soldiers drew rein and watched as Johnny and Picker disappeared over a rolling prairie ridge, heading west.

Joseph Schill
Vogelbacher Settlement
Clarion County, Pennsylvania

Dear Joseph,

I am continuing on to California to find my fortune in gold, but I could never expect to obtain the wealth in gold that I have in wisdom and knowledge over these past few months.

I no longer feel the demand for adventure and excitement that compelled me to launch that raft into the Allegheny River with little regard for the feelings of others or of my own welfare.

It was not that I was expressing bravery, for to be brave one must have knowledge of danger. I had none.

Please convey to Fr. Slattery that my faith in God, though shaken at times, has remained. It is because of that faith I know, all will be well in the end.

Your friend,
Johnny Farrell
October 1852